MW00914034

Conjuring Maud

Conjuring Maud

by Philip Danze

GreyCore Press

Cover Painting by Linda Paul, www.lindapaul.com
Cover and Text Design by Kathleen Massaro

Danze, Philip.
    Conjuring Maud / Philip Danze
    p. cm.
    LCCN 2001-086273
    ISBN 0-9671851-3-0

    1. Gold mines and mining—Africa, West—Fiction.
2. Africa, West—Fiction. 1. Title

PS 3554.A5838C66 2001   813'.6
                                 QB101-700240

Acknowledgements

I wish to thank the following people: Ray Cocoros for his influence during my formative years when he opened a door into the world of literature; Liz Nix, wherever she is, for her wise counseling; Polly Lindenbaum for discovering worth in this story and then finding a way to make it happen; and Joan Schweighardt, who really is beyond thanks with her wealth of patience, sagacity, enthusiasm and good cheer.

Also, I owe my thanks to my family: Dee, for keeping body and soul together; Philip, for his general support; Jeff, for showing me the way into this strange MAC world; and Leo for being there through the empty years.

$\mathcal{A}$lthough this is a work of fiction, certain liberties have been taken with several of the characters who are based on real people. Maud King, for instance, is patterned on Mary Kingsley, the eminent British explorer. While I have provided Maud with a few life experiences that her historical counterpart did not share, I have tried to remain true to her remarkable spirit and her indomitable dedication to the tribes of West Africa.

Chapter One

It was nothing more than a worn copy of Marcus Aurelius' *Meditations*, a slim volume extracted from a threadbare jacket hanging in a closet that I hadn't worn in forty years. And yet when I thumbed through its musty, silky pages and read the inscription inside the cover, "To Sam, with my warmest regards," signed "Cecil," my boyhood days in South Africa slowly rolled back on me and I recalled that land of intense sunlight with its deep valleys and its great walls of rock, its early morning frosts in winter and the belts of fog in the summer. The book had belonged to my father, a memento from his halcyon days. It was a gift from Cecil Rhodes, the African Empire builder.

My father's original calling was that of a doctor, and Rhodes had been his patient. For a time anyway. Before I was born. I will not venture to guess what any man's real calling is (or if there even is such a thing as a real calling). I say this because many of us entertain all sorts of grand illusions about what we can accomplish and sometimes in the interests of a very particular illusion, we go so far as to repudiate our original calling, chuck it, so to speak, after years of its having earned us a living, only to realize afterward that we had misjudged our talent and penitently ended up earning our bread by the sweat of our brow. Act in haste, they say, repent at leisure. Yes, that is how it was with my father, though he would never have admitted it. With him it was only a matter of bad luck.

He was an Australian who had gone to South Africa during the Kimberley diamond rush of the 1870s. In those days the trek from Cape Town to the mine was a grueling three months on horseback, and when he got there he rented a small shack on the perimeter of the mine itself, the pit it was called, and hammered a sign over its door: Doctor Samuel Unger.

It was a shallow dish, the pit, about a mile in diameter, and its diamonds were hidden in a soft yellow clay that was hauled to the surface in buckets, washed in cradle screens and pounded with hammers. Later, machines reached into the pit's lower blue rock strata and, of course, the roads that crossed that ever-deepening pit routinely caved in, and there were mud rushes and land slips and falling masses of rock— reefs, they were called—and hardly a day went by that Doc Unger wasn't summoned to the pit's interior to help drag out a miner crushed under a ton of stone.

Worse yet, though, were the free-for-alls. In those days a blade in the back or a bullet in the head often settled the miners' property disputes. It was more than a mine, the pit, it was a greedy Saturnalian monster that fed on human suffering. It was hotter than the Sahara at noon and as cold as a Siberian wasteland at night. At dawn, seething vapors rose from its shadowy bowels.

But the diamonds were there like no other place on earth. My father, in fact, was often tempted to buy a claim. But he didn't. How would it look, a doctor speculating? Not that he didn't invest; he did—in properties, the safe kind, in prime real estate, mostly. And sure enough, when South African land values soared, he prospered, ordered his shirts and suits from London, and married a banker's daughter. Lydia was my mother's name.

His crowning joy was the house he built, a grand house, a stone house on a hill that he felt would stand forever. It was situated in a grove of mahogany trees far from the pit with its wearying, pounding din and its ant-like activity. The house had seventeen rooms and a winding staircase and a crystal chandelier that my mother had bought at a London auction. The chandelier hung in a spacious center hall, and outside the house the grounds were guarded by large African hunting dogs that raced back and forth behind an iron spear fence.

That much I was told; I myself experienced none of this. I was told also that my father's practice grew and he lived comfortably in the world of his peers, the Rothschilds, the De Beers and a young tubercular, bookish Cape Town official named Rhodes.

Now this Rhodes fellow had emerged from the pit a very wealthy individual. His partner, Barney Barnato, was a small brisk man who wore a bowler hat. At least that is what he wore in the pictures I saw of him. An ex-boxer he was, and an aspiring actor too, with a talent for fast talk. One afternoon this Barnato scampered up to the house on the hill where Rhodes and my father were playing billiards. His face was shiny with sweat and he was out of breath.

"Speak up, man," said Rhodes impatiently, for he hated his game interrupted. And Barnato, his stiff collar soiled with the pit's yellow mud, unfolded a handkerchief and placed a dark blue stone on the billiard cloth.

"This will do my talkin' for me," he said.

Rhodes picked up the stone and examined it carefully.

"Straight from the deep ground and as fine a gem as you'll find." That's what the small man said.

Rhodes smiled as he poured three vermouths from a decanter. The stone was a blue diamond and, as Barnato had said, as fine a one as likely to be found anywhere. It glowed like a burning ember.

"There's no time to lose," said Rhodes' partner with dark, rapacious eyes. "We should buy out everyone's claim right now and amalgamate the mine. Don't you agree?"

There was a clinking of glasses, then a pensive Rhodes said to his partner: "You buy out the claims, Barney. I'm heading north. Sam here says I need a change of scenery. But I'll be back."

Rhodes had something in mind more important than diamonds.

He was an odd bird actually, this Rhodes. For one thing, he had a hankering for an Oxford degree. In fact, it was more than that; it was an obsession. For years, no matter where he was, he returned to England and registered at Oxford. I'm not sure he had to attend classes, probably not. But this time was the exception; he didn't go to England. The greater good that supercedes all else had laid its claim on him. In Rhodes' case, it was his 'grand vision.' He loaded an oxcart with provisions, and with a carbine in the crook of his arm, rode northward toward the center of Africa in as solitary a journey as was ever made by a civilized man.

He traveled for months on end, fifteen, twenty miles a day through vast spaces of barely occupied land. He was gone so long his friends and family became alarmed, then despaired of ever seeing him again; it seemed that once the jungle had closed in behind him, he had disappeared from the face of the earth.

Everyone knew he had headed north, but I don't think they knew exactly why he went. My father, though, he knew. Rhodes had confided in him once that as a lad he had learned—from reading Aristotle—that the noble life seeks the highest objective on which to exercise the highest activity of the soul. High-sounding words, yet I suspect that this was what his journey northward was all about. It had nothing to do with compass points; the compass be damned. It was an inward journey that Rhodes made. And despite the mud, the malaria and the blistering heat, I'm convinced he was after a kind of nobility, his own holy grail.

In that tubercular chest of his he clamored for what he deemed the highest objective in life to match the most profound stirrings of his soul. It was almost as if he were guided by an invisible hand.

Meanwhile, back in Kimberley, his partner Barnato went

about the dirty business of getting the miners to sell their claims—and a dirty business it was. I can see him now, a small, agile fellow in a three-button suit and that bowler of his, stalking the rim of the great Kimberley mine, and with the African sun marching across the sky like a barbarous master, lowering himself into the infamous pit to confront some bewildered miner leaning against a bed face like a tired animal.

"You've 'it bedrock, can't you see that, mon?" he'd say. "Sign off, why don't you? 'Ave you no family back 'ome? I'll make it worth your while."

The poor exhausted miner, shirtless and laboring under the sun's brutal lash, would bend over the hard blue rock which no pickaxe could bust in a productive manner and wipe the grime from his brow with a broad red handkerchief.

"Are you talkin' 'ard cash?" the miner would say, knowing he'd someday regret the moment at hand.

"'Ard cash it is," and Barney would brush his thumb across the top of a wad of bills, "and you name your own price, mon. God knows you've earned it, two years in this 'ere 'ole."

The sweaty miner might give another useless jab at the bedrock with his pick and know again in his secret heart that he had never been meant to be rich. Better set a price, he'd think and be done with it. And so he would join the many others that had signed off.

And that's how it went; whether Barney cornered them in the pit, or snuggled up to them in a saloon, or even approached them under a shadowy staircase somewhere, the miners and the little man would set a price. Sometimes the more desperate would accept a price so low as to barely take them back home (the fare to Cape Town in itself was forty pounds). But there were those who were stubborn or who had already found a bit of diamond, and they fetched upwards of four thousand pounds, a tidy sum even now for two years' work. And there would be Barney peeling out the cash and stuffing it in the miner's dusty pocket.

"I'll pick up your deed in the mornin'," he'd say.

And that would be it. They'd be gone, the lot of them. Some miners stayed on and Barney hired them to run the machines—the steam-winding engines, the puddling troughs stirred by revolving combs, the bucket elevators—for it was machinery mining that Barnato had in mind. Imagine, though, those poor miners scooping out buckets of diamonds from claim they once owned, how they'd curse their unlucky stars.

As for shrewd Barnato, he knew Rhodes would be back just as surely as you know you've got ten fingers. And he was right; after eight months, Rhodes returned from his journey. My father said it was nothing short of a physical miracle that he survived that long in the wilderness. But of course there's more to people than their physical selves. The spirit too counts for something, and though Rhodes' journey had taxed his frail body to an incredible degree, it had rejuvenated his spirit. When he returned to Kimberley, he was as a man reborn.

Barney Barnato, meanwhile, had bought out over four

hundred stake holders. He had truly made the amalgamation of the Kimberley mine a reality. Rhodes was impressed, but he retained a detached air. He was now richer than Croesus, but the mere accumulation of money didn't seem to impress him. It wasn't money he was thinking about.

For one thing, he was often seen on the streets with members of the Kimberley and Cape Ministries, and he spent a good deal of time in the mapmaker's office. For weeks on end his cottage lights shone deep into the night. Finally he asked my father if he could use the grand house on the hill "to give a very special party."

And so the prominent men of Kimberley gathered one evening and stood under my mother's glittering chandelier and then retreated to the billiard room where old friends shook hands and aperitifs were served on trays by black servants wearing white gloves. When the time came, the men sat around my father's broad dinner table and a quiet candle-lit dinner was served, the finest of everything, complete with fine wines and a wondrous choice of desserts.

While the distinguished array of guests relaxed, the Rothchilds and the De Beers among them, the host of the grand affair stood up and spoke in a clear ringing voice of what he had seen in his travels to the north. He spoke of a vast empire to be carved out of the jungles beyond the Shashi River, of another El Dorado, of fertile soils and large lakes and rivers, of a land resplendent with every resource known to man, especially gold, silver and diamonds.

He flourished maps of the Bechuanaland, the Matabele

and the Mashona lands, and he spoke of settling this great region with two thousand pioneers. The seated guests bent forward in their chairs. It wasn't only the fine wines from my father's table that went to their heads that evening.

"All types of men are needed," he said. "Mechanics, engineers, farmers and men handy with a rifle." The Boers and the Portuguese, he knew, were sure to protest. But carry on they would under the protection of the British flag, and if successful, Britain would rule the mighty north and south axis of Africa and guarantee any of Her Majesty's subjects passage from Cape Town to Cairo.

"There is no greater calling," he told them, "than our obligation to the Crown!"

Hard-boiled men they were, each in his own way, worldly men with large amounts of money and eager to make more— because in the race for power it is never the last who strives the hardest to achieve. The last strives hardly at all and is content to have bread on his table. But the second runners strive the hardest, for they wish to be first. Rhodes knew this and flung out his proposition:

The pioneers themselves would receive three thousand acres in the Masonaland and fifteen claims in the gold fields, and a company would be formed to administer the venture.

"You are my selected few," he said to the men who had all shared in the great wealth of the Kimberley mine, who were rich, adventurous types. "You are my boon companions, and I call on each of you to a glory beyond any wealth you have thus far known. I summon you to the founding of a nation!"

He only needed their pledge. They had one week to decide.

My father said British reserve was thrown to the wind, and under a hail of toasts and a tumultuous applause, every man present pledged right on the spot.

As for Rhodes, he stood there silent, imperial, his hand raised, knowing that the illustrious moment for which he been born had arrived. His still eyes shone brightly. He had at last found the highest objective to match the profound stirrings of his soul. He was on the eve of transforming his most personal need into a larger ambition and making that ambition serve an even larger cause: Britain's world dominance. The inner need, the large ambition and the final great cause were welded into one, into a sacred trinity, and Rhodes served this trinity to the end of his life as one would a god.

My father, however, did not become a shareholder in Rhodes' dream. He wanted very much to join, but my mother didn't want to live in the wilds for as long as it would take.

In time, as Rhodes predicted, his "selected few" were among the wealthiest and most powerful people in the Empire, tycoons, everyone of them. And my father, he still mended bones and taught young mothers how to burp their infants. But the pleasure he took in his ministrations was not so great anymore.

They say lightning never strikes twice in the same place. This time it did. In '86 gold was discovered in Johannesburg. Was it any wonder then that my father mortgaged his house on the hill with its crystal chandelier and its mahogany staircase, the stone house he had built to last forever, and that he withdrew his savings and bought land and land-moving equipment that would reach into the ground for the riches that had long been denied him?

The gold rush was far more important than the diamond rush had been. Gold was the very stuff of money, money needed to expand the world's industrialization. And one thing my father knew was that the gold buried deep in the Johannesburg fields, hidden deeper than even the diamonds had been, like some divine loot, belonged to the man with the machines. Rhodes and Barnato had taught him that much. And so, with the machines he bought, he started to dig, just as Rhodes and Barnato had done. It was a vast operation that he undertook, just as was the operation that Rhodes and Barnato had undertaken. Only he forgot to have their luck.

I was born in a miner's shack on the banks of the Val River. It took less than a year for my father to go broke, and even after he did, for years he still hoped to strike it rich and return to Kimberley and buy back his house on the hill. He even had hopes of resuming his practice; he kept his medical books behind a glass shelf so the dry dust would not soil their pages. In time, though, a great darkness came over him. The shack miners had no money to pay for his services and first he worked for free and then not at all.

He had fallen from a doctor to a gold speculator, and then finally he was only another miner working for wages and no amount of good fellowship could undo the loss he felt, and there was great bitterness by then between my father and his banker's daughter of a wife. And one bright morning my mother announced that she was going to visit her sister in Bloemfontein, a trip of several days. But she never arrived at Bloemfontein, and she did not return to our house. When my father told me my mother had disappeared in the bush, I felt as if my heart had been pierced. I was ten years old.

There had always been a gulf between my father and me, and now that gulf was greater, and filled with long periods of silence. There were times my father left the house for days, only to return and smack his fists into his palms and drink Cape brandy straight from a bottle.

One day I found him lying in a stupor before the fireplace. On the iron grate were charred pieces of an old photo of my mother. Nowhere in the house was there another picture of her. He had burned her out of our lives. I wondered then whether she had really disappeared in the bush. Or was she still alive? For months I agonized over this question. If she had been killed in the bush, then she was dead and time would wash away the pain. But if she were still alive somewhere, then her absence from me was deliberate and freely chosen and this kind of pain, slowly mixing with anger, was a pain that would never wash away. It could only feed the great angry silence between my father and me until it would be impossible to live with.

When I turned twelve my father sent me to a military school. I believe he was relieved to be rid of me.

Chapter Two

Predicting the course of one's life is like the drawing of an arc. Once the line has been started, it's easy to imagine its completion. Speaking for myself, I certainly had been headed in a given direction. From the age of twelve to seventeen I attended the Craighill Naval Academy, stationed on the island of Fernando Po, off the coast of Cameroon in Equatorial West Africa. The academy itself was a relic of a former British naval station set up to curb Portuguese slave trading. Upon graduation, I imagined, I'd travel the watery part of the world a bit, then marry a superior's daughter and accept a post in Johannesburg and quietly settle in to a life of domesticity. But it didn't work out that way.

I met Maud while I was still a cadet at the academy. Maud King was a famous woman in her day. Her name appears in all the encyclopedias. She was spoken of in the same breath as Stanley and Livingstone, Speke, Burton and Mungo Park. She knew Henry James very well. The British Museum once devoted an entire wing to her work.

I was sixteen years old at the time, and every Saturday morning it was my job to travel by launch and pick up the school's mail at the Cameroon postal station on the Sanaga

River. My launch was a twenty-one footer, v'd at the bow and flat at the stern. It looked like a soda pop stand with a fringed surrey canvas roof stuck on four poles. Somehow it got fitted with a Daimler gas engine, more powerful than its original motor—an Olfedt two-horse naphtha—and then nothing on any West African river could match it for speed. At full throttle it hit forty knots, and the beauty of it was that it could navigate in four feet of swamp if need be. It had been an academy boat for years until it was—quite foolishly—deemed unseaworthy. And so, one day I planted my Henry-Martini carbine (every South African youth had one) under a loose deck plank and made the boat my own. Land's End, I called it.

From Fernando Po I came each Saturday morning, bouncing on the Atlantic's waves, the sun, not yet sky-borne over the mountains—just a promise of light, barely managing to spread a muted amber glow on the dark waters—the top of Mt. Clarence sparkling with the morning's first rays. On the mainland was a narrow strip of beach where white waves broke soundlessly under a dark, misty plateau. Above it were rugged mountains that stretched arc-like across the country.

As I entered the harbor, the strengthening sun would thin out the fog and the western end of the arc of the volcanic Mt. Cameroon would appear, a rising, majestic mass whose uppermost peak was always encircled with clouds. How bold that mountain stood, planted at the edge of the sea like that, with the waves gnawing at its base, as if it were drawing a line against the sea itself—or against the sea gods, telling them:

You have come this far; you've bitten into the hard crust of Africa, but I, Mt. Cameroon, 13,000 feet high, defy you to come any further. No other African mountain challenges the sea the way Mt. Cameroon does.

And the sea gods seem to pay it tribute. It's the rainiest region in the entire world. Four-hundred plus inches of rain the mountain receives from its old tormentor. For when the Sahara sun is high, the winds blow up from the south and rain comes to the mountain's gorgeous slopes and its primeval trees grow hundreds of feet tall and are studded with orchids and arums, parasitic growths of flowers on a clubby spike, and the entire middle region of the mountain is girdled with tree ferns of great beauty.

One Saturday morning, having brought my launch to the mainland as usual, I stood in my white cadet uniform on the Sanaga bank and watched as the mail boat appeared, a large smoke-puffing sardine can coming down a molasses-thick, brackish dark river, with birds circling in its wake. As it snaked among the weeping mangroves full of the jargon of monkeys, among trees that in their interlocking greenery all but blotted out the sun, it tooted its whistle to part the water of herds of gleaming hippos bathing in its path. On the far shore teams of basking crocodiles hardly stirred.

The boat was soon secured to a tree and swarthy, unshaven, hard-drinking traders came stomping off a gang-plank to a rickety dock; a missionary was fast on their heels.

Then Maud appeared, a tall, slender white woman, her arms loaded with books and a small monkey on her shoulder.

She wore a bonnet and a white blouse held inside a skirt by a broad belt. Behind her was her carrier, a large black man in European dress, stepping smartly with an ivory cane in his right hand while balancing a trunk on his broad opposite shoulder. He came down the gangplank with an indisputable air of the authority that had been conferred on him, it seemed, by two simple adornments—a captain's sea cap and a snake rib through his nose.

I thought Maud might be a temperance missionary at first. Then I saw the holstered revolver that hung at her side. When she came close, I offered to help with her books and she thanked me.

That she was beautiful did not occur to me at the time. Her peeled and freckled face was lean. She had a firm mouth and chin and blondish locks. Her blue eyes were kind, but sad; all the world's woes seemed to reside in them—even when she smiled. I found myself wondering if maybe she had lost a child—if this was the great sadness that hid her beauty.

Perhaps it was that sadness that I was drawn to; I can't say. But I recall that after we introduced ourselves and spoke a few words, I said, "Perhaps I will see you again." I wanted very much to see her again.

"Perhaps," she said. "I'm always on the river."

"I'll be glad to bring you your mail," I said. My boldness startled me. My voice seemed strange, as if I were listening to someone else talking. How aware I was that I had yet to put a razor to my face.

"That's very kind of you," she said, and her eyes filled with the seeds of curiosity.

We spoke for a moment longer. She was on her way to Victoria, she said, a nearby town, to pick up an order of cotton from England. And while she was there, she had shopping to do. She collected samples for the British Museum and needed nets and specimen bottles.

I would learn later that Maud King was a trader. She bartered with the natives—colorful cottons from the mills of England for rubber, ivory and palm oil. But the trading business was mostly a ruse. It brought her closer to the tribes, and that was her real intention. Her true calling was that of an ethnologist, as her father had been in his later years, and it was her hope to one day complete his great unfinished book about the West African tribes.

There is no accounting for people's decisions. Perhaps our feelings and actions are no more than the workings of some divine puppeteer. Maud King could have stayed in England and lived on her family estate, hosting her weekend guests, tending her garden and singing in the church choir. But she had decided not to.

Certain people at the time of decision are strong and willing to gamble their entire lives, throw away old friendships, burn every bridge, take on the most strenuous course in school, move to a distant land. In time they achieve whatever it is they're after, to live without children, or a wife, or a husband, to give themselves entirely to a new career, the Foreign Service, the convent or even, as in Maud King's case, a life in Equatorial West Africa.

Once they achieve their objective, however, the fire goes out of them and they wither. The strength it took to attain their goal leaves them and they sink into their own routine; the vivid coloring of the life they chose starts to fade, and the years pass and ultimately that moment of decision is only a memory.

When I first met Maud her eyes were sad, like the dying embers of a once great fire.

After that first day, Maud referred to me as her mailman, because no matter how far up the river she camped, there I was, every Saturday morning as I had promised, with her mail, mostly letters from relatives and friends, bank statements and scientific journals. She tried to discourage me from making those long solitary trips. But after a while, she seemed to look forward to my visits.

Actually, we had much in common. Her father, like mine, had been a doctor, and also somewhat of a capricious adventurer. In his youth he had gone to Australia in search of gold—while my father had left Australia and ended up searching for gold in Africa. A regular Flying Dutchman her father was though, prancing about the four continents as the constant companion of hypochondriac sultans or marquises, attending their nosebleeds and hiccups, their migraines and their indigestions. His globe hoppings were a kind of distraction, no doubt. Just what it was he wanted to be distracted from I can only guess. Perhaps it was to get away from his sickly wife, languishing in their country home at Kent, or perhaps simply to see more of the world than a London medical practice would allow.

At any rate, he came to see himself as an ethnologist as well as a doctor. But the real difference between Maud's father and mine was that my father had come to ruin, while hers, despite his carefree, whimsical nature, had left her a manor house at Crossgate in Kent, as well as a pension.

And a ring. I mustn't forget the ring. The old boy had given it to her when she was eight or nine. He told her it had belonged to an African king and had magical powers. An ivory ring, it was, inset with gold, and three sizes too large for her. She cherished it all the same.

For years, she said, whenever he was away from home, and she was lonely, caring for her sick mother, she'd wish on her ring for her father's return and sure enough, in time he'd show up, a bit older, a bit wiser. After he died, the ring allowed her to believe a part of her father was still with her, protecting her, so to speak.

As for her pension, it wasn't much, about three hundred pounds a year, just enough to get by on. When her mother died, she visited Africa, was enthralled with everything about it, returned to London, got a job as a trader and returned to Africa on a more or less permanent basis. Her widowed cousin, Rita Anthony King, a writer of children's books, occupied her house. It was a good arrangement. Better that someone should live in the house and care for it than it should go to rot. That was Maud's thinking. She had no use for it anyway, once she discovered Africa.

I made up my mind when I heard this that I would give Maud something that would be useful to her. And I knew what it would be. I had once chided her about her bonnet. It offered no protection against the sun or the mosquitoes and needed a strong soaking every night.

"Listen here, mailman," she said, "it's all I have."

That very week I went to Douala, a large coastal town, where bold Jack crows perched on iron gates and the tribes of the Sudan strolled the streets with their turbans and flowing gowns. There I entered a French shop and bought a brimmed straw hat with an attachable mosquito net and had it packed in a large box.

The following Saturday, well before that old dark sun struggled to surmount the mainland's eastward mountains, I churned up the Sanaga with my bow lights shining brightly.

Deep into Bantu country I went, among the Adouma people. Maud was outside her tent that misty dawn writing at a table. I tiptoed up behind her and placed the box on the table.

"Lord's sake," she said opening it. "Where on earth did you get this? It must have cost you a half year's allowance. Really, Davey."

"Put it on," I said. She had traveled for three years with experienced men of the world, hard bargainers, coasters, administrators, colony men all of them, and though some had sought to know her better, none had ever given her a gift, she said. I was very pleased to hear that, though of course I didn't say so. She removed the bonnet and tried on her new straw hat. "How does it look?"

Lightheaded as I felt just then, I reached forward and slanted it, so that a sheltering shade crossed her brow. The mosquito net gave her an air of mystery. I told her it looked fine. She hurried into her tent and returned with a hand mirror.

"You shouldn't have spent your money on me, the price of things these days. Lord knows." Yet she turned her head from side to side in a coquettish manner, her face beaming, and for a moment that sadness I was used to seeing in her eye was absent.

"There's no one I'd rather spend my money on," I said, lowering my head.

She sighed. "You're a dear lad, Davey." And she kissed me on the cheek as one might a brother, and the place burned where her lips touched my face, and I knew then beyond a shadow of a doubt that I was in hopelessly in love with her.

I called her Ma, as the natives did. She was sixteen years my senior.

One day I handed her a letter from her cousin, Rita Anthony, and watched while she read it. It seemed to put her in a thoughtful mood. It was just before nightfall on the eve of a big holiday. I asked her what she was really looking for in Africa.

The darkening jungle throbbed with the beat of drums. High in the mahogany trees the Colobus monkeys glided from limb to limb. Below them were the swallow tails, the hornbills, and the soft glow of an owl in flight. Lower down the leopard and the python waited, while the gorilla silently roamed the forest floor.

"It's the African personality I'm after," she said. "Lord's sakes, Davey, out there are thousands of miles of unexplored jungle. God knows how many tribes, each with a different custom. A deserving light is what it needs, this dark illusion we call Equatorial West Africa."

She gestured to the mud huts in the center of the clearing. "You think these people are the children the Darwinists say they are? Or maybe the devils the missionaries imagine? They have survived in this white man's grave by being respectful of the laws of nature."

Her face darkened and her chin grew as firm as a clenched fist.

"But because they don't build railroads or manufacture Enfields, they are smashed into a European mold and a Crown tax put on their land. A tribesman works all year to pay it off, only to face the same tax the next year. It's bloody unfair. It's slavery. No wonder the Union Jack's called the butcher's bloody apron!"

"Liverpool's hired assassin," she once told me Parliament had called her. She had attacked the colonial interests through the Crown Colony Bureau.

"They'll crucify you, Ma," I said. "They'll throw up to you that you've traded in gin."

Her voice quivered. "I've never traded anything I was ashamed of. My gin was better than any local toddy. Ask Surah Am. And if the tribes want a holiday and want to wear smart clothes, where's the harm?"

"They'll say you foster polygamy."

"That's missionary rubbish. Sakes alive, Davey, West Africa's double the size of Europe and badly under-peopled. The missionaries are a bunch of Judas goats that lead the tribes to the slaughter. No dancing, no singing, no wearing of smart clothes, no tom-toms. Sanctimonious rot! Scratch a skinny missionary, I say, and you'll find a paunchy lumber tycoon!"

Once she got started there was no stopping her.

"Davey, don't you see, the one thing that keeps this land from being totally raped is the fetish. Once the fetish goes, there goes Africa."

The fetish was a belief that everything in nature—trees, animals, river—has a soul, and is therefore equal to man. The fetish saw material things as sacred and linked to the gods beyond, and protected by them. The fetish made the tribes people feel a part of a holy nature.

"It's important, Davey," she said, "that the tribes keep this belief. It's their moral compass. Without it they would lose their spiritual bearings and become as despondent in the jungle as the white man is. The missionaries think they are christianizing the tribes, but they are simply destroying the tribes' religion so the paunchy colonials can make free use of their land, chop down their trees, build logging roads and all the rest. And that's the bloody truth, because once a tree's not sacred anymore, why not chop it down? And who's going to stop them? The almighty British Empire, where the sun never sets and the blood never dries? Judas goats! It makes my blood boil when I think if it."

"I've survived without the fetish," I said in the hope of draining her anger.

The tom-toms were beating strongly, like the pounding heart of the jungle itself, and a circle of tribesmen had already started passing lit torches in preparation for the tribal dance. Above the green darkness of the forest floor we could hear the elephants roaming among the buttresses of the giant trees.

She turned to me. "Perhaps you've found your own reason for living."

I had, but there was nothing to be gained by mentioning it.

In my comings and goings with Maud's mail, I came to know Surah Am. He was a bright fellow, and Maud depended on him a lot. He was her all-around porter, her guide and her foreman, and as he commanded a wide range of native dialects, he was also her interpreter. He was of the Niksek people, and the snaked rib he wore through his nose was to ward off evil spirits. The sea captain's hat was simply for the authority it conferred. His ivory-handled cane, he believed, guaranteed him luck.

Like most Africans of that day, he believed in sorcery and was a man of many secrets. Secrets, he once told me, made a man strong inside. A man without secrets was a weakling at the table of his superiors, willing to please, a happy-faced fool. This was fine thinking, I thought—until Maud one day told me that Surah Am learned most of his secrets from spiders.

She told me that he believed spiders could talk and were immensely worth listening to. They told him that the Evil One was afraid of iron, that certain trees were haunted at night, that the best thing to do when a cow stopped giving milk was to have her owner urinate on her. He also knew which roots and herbs revived virility and of the many kinds of charms to protect one from knives and guns. He learned from the spiders that a man would become rich if he plucked a single hair from a prostitute's head. And above all, he learned that a wise man avoids straight lines, for evil spirits follow straight lines.

"One thing about Surah Am," said Maud with a laugh, "he doesn't live a dull life."

Chapter Three

That spring I did not see Maud during my end-term period; I was too busy with final exams. But I had written my father that once my finals were out of the way, I was going to stay with a friend for a while before returning home to Johannesburg.

"Don't wander too far," my father wrote back. "The Zulus are smarting for a fight."

My father had often spoken of the Zulu kings, of Chatka and Umpanda. As a doctor he had attended King Cetswayo, and he had heard the great king's dying words: "I hear the sound of the feet of a great white people. They will tread this land flat." And there were the stories of the twelve hundred British soldiers slain by the Zulus at Isandhwana and of the bloody reprisal at Ulandi. Little did I realize that before the summer was over, Zulu spears would be hurled at the hearts of British soldiers.

In Central Africa the rainy season runs from January to April; that year it continued into May. But with that special enthusiasm that only the young can muster, I finished my exams and headed my launch for the African mainland. When I reached a few miles beyond the river's mouth, well into the jungle, the rain-fed river had widened to the point that it spilled over into a vast flood plain, a swamp actually, broken by hundreds of muddy, thickly-wooded islands, a very beautiful sight—if you're not trying to navigate through it.

First off, there were crocodiles. It was astonishing how they could spring off such short, crusty legs. There were also trapped civets and leopards, restlessly pacing the lower limbs of trees above their watery surroundings. Herds of hippos waded among the islands or crossed the land with such grace that under different circumstances, I might have marveled that such thin crusts of dry earth could have supported the weight of their ponderous bodies.

But neither the cats nor the hippos bothered me as much as the crocodiles did. I removed my Martini-Henry from under the deck plank and held it in the crook of my arm. The crocs, stirred by the hum of my engine, slipped silently from the islands into the water, their long dark shadows under the murky surface betraying their sinister presence.

My compass was useless; it could guide me eastward into the jungle's interior, but it could not tell me the water's depth—and I needed to know that, for if the Land's End ran aground, I couldn't enter the water and push her back into the main channel, not with so many crocs about.

Nevertheless, I trolled upstream, trying to stay within the arching trees that formed a broad avenue through the jungle. Air bubbles rose from the flooded ground and long rope-like vines hung listlessly into the gleamless water. I moved slowly through an amber light that filtered down from the high green darkness above as if through an endless procession of stained glass windows, and my engine droned beneath the vast canopies of the tree tops in the way an organ's sounds rebound beneath a cathedral's vaulted ceiling.

Luck was with me. True, I had lost lots of time, drifting here and there, but by late afternoon I had found my way back to the main channel, and when the river narrowed again, I passed several abandoned trading stations and rows of reed huts facing the river. Not a sign of life. Toward dusk I knew I could not reach Maud's camp by sundown, and so I started looking for a likely place to spend the night. Any one of those abandoned trading posts would have served my purpose. The British, the French, the Germans and other Europeans had traded in Cameroon, especially along the Sanaga.

Soon enough I spotted another trading station, thanks to some puffs of smoke. It was a bit in from the river, on a spur, and I headed for it. I still felt lucky. After all, I had overcome a flood plain and encountered slews of crocodiles, and I was still in one piece.

I almost looked forward to this new encounter. I had only to share this person's company for the night. Perhaps I might even learn a thing or two from him. In retrospect, the flooding and the crocodiles were natural and entirely predictable. In dealing with them I had only to exercise some navigational skill and return to the river's channel. But no such simple formula could have prepared me for Monsieur Delacroix, bless his soul.

I went ashore, my Martini-Henry in hand, and almost

immediately I was aware of a stench that could only be the odor of death. Before me were two houses in a partial jungle clearing, one house just a heap of rotted, bleached wood, the other, a tin one, with boarded windows. A desolate yard in front of the houses was spiked with saplings and wild undergrowth. No garden, no fence. Only a flagpole, on which hung the tattered colors of France.

Having stood in a boat all day, I was glad to feel a bit of solid land beneath my feet. But I would have turned back from the stench, that much I can guarantee, had not the house door opened and a lone gent appeared. Just as well, I thought, at least someone to talk to.

I greeted him warmly, but, to my complete surprise, he marched straight by me, as if I were invisible, a bugle tucked under his arm. He was a haggard, shabbily-dressed fellow in his fifties, his beard unevenly shorn and his hair chopped more than cut. He stood at attention, put the bugle to his mouth and burst forth a short military call. Following the bugle's echo, he gave a sharp command and then proceeded to take down the flag. Another command and he folded the flag and placed it smartly under his arm, with the bugle. That done, he made an abrupt about-face and looked me in the eye.

"Raymond Delacroix, deputy of the Territorial Assembly," he announced with a snappy salute.

Anyone could see he was deranged. Even so, when he glanced at my rifle and at my uniform and quickly added, "I've been expecting you," I was dumbfounded.

What amazes me to this day is that I did not do an about-face. Instead, in my best classroom French, I suggested that he had me mixed up with someone else, that I only needed a place to spend the night. Considering the state of his mind, I tried not to sound too confrontational. He asked my name, and in such a way as to suggest that he was remiss in not having remembered it. I told him. He had the eyes of a man who had not slept well in years.

"Ah, yes, yes, the Governor's office said you would be along soon, Monsieur Unger." He shook my hand. "Many are called but few are chosen."

"But I'm not who you think I am," I protested.

Delacroix's smile suggested a deep satisfaction with the worldly order of things. "Who of us is, Monsieur Unger?" he said. "Let us go inside. You should meet the prisoner. Relax, Monsieur Unger, formalities in the tropics make one tired. I will bring you food, some wine."

I was tired and hungry, and at a loss as to how to handle this lunatic. When he swept his arm invitingly toward his dilapidated house that seemed to stand in defiance of time and which sank into the shadows as he spoke, I crossed a shaky porch and followed him.

We entered into a large, but dingy room. An oil lamp was already lit. There was a table and three chairs, one of which was a rocker, and a cupboard. A rifle leaned against a window, and a revolver in a holster hung on the wall. The room contained nothing else. The floor was pure dirt and the walls were made of reeds, probably a remnant of the original house.

"Monsieur Unger, meet Alain Dupre, our prisoner." He gestured toward the rocker.

I peered into that shadowy corner in earnest expectation that this Dupre fellow was sitting there, perhaps tied up. But the rocker was empty. Quite empty.

"Well, what have you to say for yourself, you treasonous leper?" the Deputy said to his phantom prisoner. "The Governor has sent us Monsieur Unger here to carry out your sentence. Monsieur Unger knows how to deal with your kind."

He was talking to no one, of course. God, all I needed was a place to sleep. I tried again to make him understand this.

"Of course, Monsieur Unger," he said. "Make yourself at home, and in the morning, following the raising of our flag— for however remote we are from our motherland, in our hearts we are still her children..." (lowering his voice, he completed his sentence with an appropriate tone of gravity) "...you shall execute Monsieur Dupre."

"Execute Dupre?" I was dumbfounded.

"I confess there were times I despaired of the delay and thought I might have to do it myself. I'm prepared, you know. But it's not a job for a man my age. You younger people have your careers to look after. Now, you'd better sit. I'll bring you dinner."

My protests went unheard for he immediately left the house. I had thought him harmless at first, but now I was not so sure. In the corner of the room stood the rocker, silent. It was bizarre: I was an executioner in the mind of a lunatic.

I went to the window. One thing about the tropics: Darkness never seems to linger; when it falls, it's pitch black suddenly. I couldn't see much, but I did see Delacroix standing by a fire. Then he came back, with a piece of meat on a fork. He placed it on a plate that he took from his cupboard and poured me a small glass of wine.

The meat was tasty, the wine a bit sour. Apparently the Deputy had already eaten. He sat opposite me and chided his prisoner.

"You know, Dupre, the colony will be well to be rid of you. You're worthless; not even the cannibals want you." He chuckled softly, then became stern again. "You should take your medicine like a man. Admit you are a deserter, that you are also a Dreyfusard, a follower of that infamous traitor. You've been found guilty of treason, but little does the State know you're a poacher to boot, that you've killed animals for their skins. Anyone can smell what you've done for miles around. Don't you know that running a tannery in itself is worth a good lashing? Well, have you nothing to say for yourself?"

Delacroix's shoulders sagged, his right one especially, as if he had been carrying a heavy cross; he became smaller. His brows lost their arch, his face took on a mournful expression; when he sat in the rocker a hoarse whisper escaped him, the voice of Dupre:

"The charges haven't been proven. You can execute me, but if you do, you will kill an innocent man."

The Deputy-turned-Dupre rose from the rocker with a truly remarkable transformation of his body. He became the Deputy again.

"Innocent? You think the State errs? The entire Territorial

Assembly has heard your case. Your guilt has been proven. You filthy leper, come here, we'll show Monsieur Unger what you've done."

The Deputy Delacroix pulled the imaginary Dupre out of the rocker and dragged him to the door. I rose, my rifle in hand. "Come Monsieur Unger," he said. "You must see what this leprous dog has been up to." He pushed Dupre into the night and ordered him to march toward the tin house. I followed; better that, I thought, than be left alone in the house while a madman wandered about outside. The Deputy and Dupre and I entered the tin house. The odor matched the heat: Both were absolutely unbearable.

An oil lamp was lit and I immediately saw what Delacroix referred to as a "shameful sight." On one wall were the bloody rotting carcasses of large animals. They had been hooked through their chins or through their ankles and stripped of their hides, their dumb eyes fixed in a stare. On a long table were chips of tanning bark and salt and a pile of organs, hearts, lungs and livers. Milky brains had been placed in shallow pans and allowed to soak in some kind of solution for God knows what reason. On the adjacent wall were the hides of these animals, the most gorgeous furs imaginable, lush pelts of leopards and tigers, of springbok and wildebeest, kudus and a large variety of smaller mammals. It was as if this madman had skinned these animals of their very souls.

"How do you explain this, you leper?" the Deputy demanded. Dupre sulked. "Well? Answer. Have you lost your tongue? Monsieur Unger, you can see for yourself, the evidence is abundant. The absolute shame of what this man has done."

I nodded. There was indeed a small fortune in this boarded-up tin house.

"Well, tomorrow it will be finished. But not forgotten! The State will never forget your disgrace, Dupre. It has sent us your angel of death in the person of Monsieur Unger."

We returned to the house. The Deputy was by now extremely agitated and he continued to admonish poor Dupre, who, in turn, tried to defend himself. Was this for my benefit, or did this go on every night, this charade, this idiotic drama? Dupre finally confessed that he had hoped to trade the skins on the black market and retire to Paris.

"I had expected," he admitted, "to have lived out my days in that City of Light with nothing to do but stroll along the boulevards and sip brandy at the sidewalk cafes."

As sleepy as I was, I felt sorry for poor Dupre. I had heard of Europeans going mad when kept in the tropics too long. West Africa wasn't called the white man's grave for nothing. If the fever didn't get you.... Alone for months on end, on a river trading post with not a soul to talk to. Seeing the exact same scene all the time, hearing the same sounds. It's enough to drive anyone mad. Six months, a year, was all a man should be expected to work under such conditions.

Suddenly I was aware that the Deputy had asked me if the prisoner had to be blindfolded before his execution, and I said no, it was not mandatory. I had become a part of the grand charade. And should the prisoner be executed before or after breakfast? This kind of lunacy knew no bounds and long into the night it continued.

We were even joined at some point by members of the Territorial Assembly, whose accusations added to those of Delacroix. Dupre was indeed a doomed man, and as Delacroix had said, I was to be his angel of death. Did I sleep that night? I suppose I did, on and off, in a manner of speaking, mostly off, and when morning came, the rapid recitation of a bugle call awoke me.

The reed walls, the table, the three chairs were still there. But the gun holster was gone. The bugle stopped. At the open door, I leaned against the frame, my rifle in hand. The Deputy was raising the flag in the gray dawn. When it reached the top of that desolate pole, he shouted.

"Monsieur Unger!" His voice was hoarse and heavy.

I raised my hand slowly, as a school boy not wishing to be called upon.

"The State is waiting, Monsieur Unger."

I staggered forward, still half asleep, hoping to awake and find this had all been a dream. But it was no dream. The Deputy's holster was strapped to his waist and his revolver was in it. Again he told me to get ready. His voice was dry. In it I heard the cry of a dying animal.

I'd had enough. Without hesitation I staggered across the shaky porch, down the broken steps and stood out in the open, for a few moments perhaps, thinking very hard. Then I lurched past him and headed for the river. He shouted that I was the official executioner and ordered me in the name of the Territorial Assembly to come back.

"I shall report you to the Governor for dereliction of duty!" His voice was shrill now.

I waved him off and continued running. His voice reached me again, from a longer distance this time. It was charged with panic.

"I shall carry out the sentence myself! You hear, Monsieur Unger? I shall be the angel of death!"

I ran faster.

"The Governor will hear of this!" he shouted. "Your career is finished!" He continued to call me. The last dim words I heard from him were: "The State will be served!"

Through the years I've heard that declaration repeated many times in one form or another and always, it seems, by a madman. I reached my launch and unhitched it from the tree it was tied to. I was far from death's odor and the shouting of the Deputy now. I pushed out from the shore, jumped in my boat and was revving the engine when I heard the shot, a single shot.

I cut the engine and listened. Like a leopard, the sun sprang into the sky. I heard nothing more.

That morning I wanted to get as far from that post as I could. Maud's camp was a good two hours upriver. I had never traveled so deep into the interior before. Darkening masses of mahogany trees were shrouded in a profusion of vines rising from a misty forest floor reaching high into a dusky sky. Tall stands of kevazingo trees, monarchs of the rain forest with their brazen unpetalled flowers, leaped out from the shadows of the ebonies in their midst. Beyond the rapids and falls were the low, rounded Crystal Mountains, gleaming in the morning light, worn down by thousands of years of rain.

Maud was out trading when I arrived, and that was just as well. I was exhausted and needed sleep. Just before dark she returned. Her long skirt was torn and her rolled up sleeves showed elbow bruises; strands of hair had sprung from her chignon and her nails were broken.

"Hello Davey," she said as she took my hand. "God, it's so good to see you. What have you been up to? Taking finals I expect. I thought you were returning home this week."

"I've won a reprieve." I watched for any change in her expression. There was none. And so I told her about the flooded river. My time with her was so precious to me; I didn't want it spoiled by talking about gruesome matters, yet I saw no way to avoid it: I told her too about my incredibly strange night at the Frenchman's place.

"Oh, we know him," she said. "He talks to himself a lot."

"He's beyond that stage now, I'm afraid. I think he shot himself."

"Good heavens! Are you serious?"

While I explained, she slumped in a chair. "We should look into it. Tomorrow first thing, poor chap."

I sat beside her and told this trading business was wearing her down, that she needed a holiday. She allowed a small laugh. "I thought you knew, Davey, my time here has been one long holiday."

Later, over tea, she unfolded a map and pointed a broken

finger nail to a faint line, the Ogowe River in Gabon. She said no white person had ever penetrated the jungle beyond that point. It was her intention to do so. "I'm trying to get the British Museum to back an expedition."

Meanwhile there were specimens to gather, mostly fish, snakes and birds. "Actually, anything that moves." She smiled weakly, for she really did seem very tired. And photos. The museum liked photos, especially of the silverback gorillas. I offered to accompany her wherever she wanted to go, to take her in my boat. She looked at me strangely then, as if she were only just realizing that being near her was all that mattered to me, and she said that she would very much enjoy my company.

The next morning we went back to the old trading post—Maud, myself, and Surah Am and his crew. We even brought some shovels to bury the Frenchman, but damned if we could find him. He was gone, vanished like smoke. Not a sign of him, nor of anything else; his rifle, his bugle were gone. The pelts were gone, even the flag. Only my dish and glass were still on the table—the only indications that I hadn't dreamt it all up.

Maud and I quickly put the whole business behind us. I've wondered about it now and then. At the time, though, it didn't seem important. I was young, and Maud was so full of life. So there we were, Maud in her skirt, me in my rolled up trousers, traveling the waterways, shooting pictures, taking notes. I snipped plants with long scissors and pressed the leaves between paper sheets and doused them in formaldehyde. She observed that the hard fibrous tannin leaves were poisonous and untouched by the wildlife, while the smaller red leaves were riddled with holes. She was particularly interested in the species that subsisted on the nectar of flowers, the sun birds, the butterflies, the bees, the ants, the mice and the bats that fed at night.

She especially loved the sun birds. They typified Africa to her with their colorful feathers and cheerful songs. Her life force was inexhaustible and she sought out the jungle's smallest details—for instance, how the seedlings of ironwood trees grew in the gaps of the forest canopy where competing trees could not shut out the light. It was a pure joy to be in her company.

Once we were caught in a torrential rain and had to take cover under a giant mushroom and she laughingly hugged me to her side so I wouldn't get wet. Another time we were going down river in some rough water. I was for pulling the Land's End by hand; Maud wouldn't hear of it. Into the rapids we charged; the engine stalled, the boat capsized and we found ourselves tumbling downstream. As soon as we made it to shore and retrieved the empty boat, she sank to the ground laughing.

I reminded her that the equipment and the specimens were gone. I was quite put out.

"And you, Davey," she said, "look like a wet frog. Haven't you ever wanted to spill like that? Lord's sake, Davey, where's your sense of humor?" She scrambled to her feet, soaked to the skin and smelling like an old English sheepdog.

"It's all out there somewhere," she said. "Nothing's lost. Come on, Davey, let's put a good foot under us, as the Irish say, and start looking." So, back into the water we went, and as her wide skirt billowed up around her—she tried to keep it down but was unable to—she laughed all the harder. Eventually, we found most of the equipment, even most of the bottled specimens.

The next day, with a tripod camera on board the launch, we approached the blue foothills of the Crystal Mountains. Maud said the gorillas the museum wanted her to photograph lived in the tangled slopes of a grove of huge hagenia trees. But we couldn't get near the gorillas. Every time we tried, they spotted us and barked out a series of vicious hoots.

Moreover, the slopes were infested with snakes. Our boots were stout enough to withstand a ground level snake attack, but the tangled terrain made it hard to distinguish an ordinary vine from a poisonous viper that we might absentmindedly brush aside.

Maud finally decided it was too risky to continue. "There's probably an old silverback up there who'll charge just to show his subordinates he's fearless."

That night, after dinner, Maud pulled a phonograph out of her trunk and played the music of Rachmaninoff and Beethoven's *Ode to Joy*, and beyond it we could hear the grunts and sounds of an ape beating his chest. "That old silverback," said Maud. "He's probably worked up over some female." A senior silverback gorilla, she explained, was an absolute monarch. His will was law. He could have any female he wanted, but he usually preferred an experienced one and terrorized any younger male who approached her.

"And if an illicit mating should take place?" I asked.

"He'd surely kill the offspring," she said.

"What choice then do the younger ones have?"

"Not much. They can wait for the old boy to die or be killed off by a rival. Or they can kidnap females from other groups. It's risky, but it works. It's called brute force." A low laugh escaped her. "We British have been getting away with it for centuries."

She took me to the Eshrivas people once. She knew the rivers and the mountains like the back of her hand and had a remarkable command of tribal tongues. At the time we witnessed a celebration of the full moon. The tom-toms beat rapidly and the tribesmen and their women faced each other and pumped their knees in frank imitation of the sex act. Maud was emancipated in many ways, yet there was still an impenetrable Victorian core to her being, and she turned from me to cover her embarrassment.

We visited other tribes too, and they treated her royally and always wanted to trade. Her main interest of course was in learning their laws and customs. She was endlessly jotting in a notebook. Her trading, as I already mentioned, was simply a way of approaching the villages. Sometimes when she had nothing to trade, no more cloth or fish hooks or combs or toothbrushes, she'd wave the tribesmen off.

"No business today," she'd laugh. Finally, though, she'd

trade her own personal belongings, her blouses and stockings, anything to stay among these people. She loved Africa, and that was the difference between us. Although I had been born in Africa, I felt myself an intruder, a white person in a black man's land. But she didn't feel that way at all. She felt she belonged there, that she was one of them, in her soul, where it counted.

West Africa was a strange land of sublime beauty, of violence and sorcery, of amber, gold, silver and ivory, of scarred faces and beaded bodies. It was also grotesque, but Maud saw a divine intelligence in everything, even in the acacia trees with their clawed branches and needle thorns. In their menacing defense she understood God perfectly, she said.

One day I accompanied her north to a somber land of yellow grass and acacia trees where we met an outcast of the Bamileke tribe. He wore a wide hat with parrot feathers, also a beaded apron and a mask with small elephant tusks. He claimed to be half-man, half-hyena. He spoke to Maud in his own dialect.

Bokomo was his name. He was a wood carver by profession but an outcast because of his laughter. His fellow tribesmen couldn't bear the sound of it—or its inappropriateness. That's what he told us. If his neighbors' crops withered, he laughed. If the buffalo failed to give milk, he laughed. He laughed at the sickness of the elderly and at the death of the newborn. And that was why the Obo, the witchdoctor, called him a hyena-man and banished him to the mountains until he could redeem himself.

"And how might that be?" Maud asked.

He removed his mask. He was a man of extreme age. His face was the blackest I'd ever seen, totally burned to a soot and covered with a network of hairline cracks, like that of a clay pot that had been left in the kiln too long. He explained that a large horde of baboons came down from the mountain caves and raided the village at night and stole the goats and raped the women, especially the chaste ones. This was bad, he explained, for a young tribesman would pay the father of a raped bride less than he would for a virgin. For this reason, the village fathers wanted the baboons killed. The Obo said that he could redeem himself by killing the baboons.

"And have you killed any?" Maud asked.

He had not. The baboons were large and each day they grew stronger. He was old and each day he grew weaker, having only berries and roots to eat.

Maud promptly gave him all the food we had, then pressed a Victoria coin into his palm. "Give your Obo this," she said, "and he will let you return to your village."

He examined the coin, his parched face drenched in a shameless glee.

"And Bokomo," Maud said with her special brand of evangelical fervor, "no more laughing at the misfortunes of others, you hear?"

His mouth widened into a toothless grin.

As we drew apart, the outcast going his way, Maud and I going ours, I had to laugh. Was he an outcast or only a shrewd beggar who had taken advantage of Maud? I asked her what divine plan was being served in being conned by this Bokomo. Maud shrugged me off with a laugh of her own.

Then, from a distance, from the amber mist surrounding Bokomo, came a weird sound, unlike any I had ever heard before. It entered my heart like a spear. Laughter? I suppose you could call it that. But I'd say it was more an anguished cry, a grotesque, never-to-be-forgotten choking cry that reached an intense howling pitch, loud with pain and pleading, an all too human cry, that for all its fullness bespoke a simple truth. Yes, yes, it said, I, Bokomo, have been banished to the caves, far from family and friends and made to survive in the sun and against the pitiless strength of baboons. But what hurts even more is life's ultimate separation, that each of us is an outcast, a frightened human shape cast down on earth as if from the sky and nothing, not food from a stranger, nor kindness, nor a Queen Victoria coin, can change that.

Maud and I were in a land without a written language, a somber, misty land where sharp needles protruded from the acacia trees, a land of yellow grass with the hills full of baboons, and here was a man whose cry (they called it laughter; maybe it was a grunt, maybe a groan, God only knows) carried the emotional weight of a King Lear. No wonder he was banished. In his heart of hearts, he was a poet, this Bokomo fellow. Under his parrot hat and weird getup, he was a poet, and even in the darkest Africa, poets can be an unsettling force. Maud's laughter subsided, and so did mine, but the hyena-man's laughter continued, for his was the wiser laughter.

Chapter Four

Later that summer Maud and I went to the coast. The air was cool there and the large luminous sky sang with the sound of the waves and the cry of the fisher hawk. At the edge of the sea we stood on the continent's last mossy rocks and walked barefoot through the sand. Then we entered the Atlantic with our clothes on and swam beyond the waves and afterward dried ourselves on boulders so thick with moss it was like lying on a bed of grass.

The dark jungle was behind us, and the line dividing the sea and the sky had all but vanished. Maud said the colonial administrators had taken advantage of the natives. "I fear for the worst," she said. "Our weekly caravans from the coast, our hard roads, our railroads. Enough. I want to see a free Africa. Not an Africa smashed into a European mold."

We walked in the sand, our shoes slung over our shoulders. "Maud," I said, "you'll run yourself ragged with the demands you make on yourself. You've been a good trader, and now you've set your mind to exploring. What will it be next year?"

I wanted her to understand that she should stop trying to give all the time and for once think of taking. But I knew it was futile asking her to do something so contrary to her nature. I also feared that whatever she did, it would take her away from me.

She stopped walking. With lowered eyes and cutting a furrow in the sand with her toe, she said, "Maybe Africa doesn't need me as much as I think. Maybe I'm the one who needs Africa."

A crown of clouds appeared over the jungle—tomorrow's rain, I thought. She touched my hand. "Africa is my husband. Don't you know that?"

We walked in silence, then we re-climbed the boulders and watched the fisher hawks from above the beach. I was wishing that I could ask her to let her hair down, when all at once—as if she could hear my thoughts, or maybe as if my thoughts could penetrate her will—she began to untie her chignon.

"I've never seen your hair down," I said.

The unknotted hair tumbled across her shoulders and more fully framed her face. She swept it to one side, exposing one ear, and her hair lay on her opposite shoulder unfurled and radiant in the sun. Then she laughed. "I suppose you'd rather I were younger."

I answered right away. "No, rather I were older."

Fisher hawks hovered overhead.

"Don't say that, Davey. We get old soon enough. Youth is the most precious possession we have."

"Not if it keeps me from you."

"Nonsense, Davey."

I waited for her to say more, but she remained silent.

We sat up there on the mossy rock, barely able to see where the blue sea ended and the blue sky began. The sun pressed down on the beach and shadows hid between piled rocks where the crawling things gathered and the scorpion slept.

We watched the arched-winged birds circling in the sky— osprey birds, she called them, fisher hawks. "My father says the Zulus are smarting for a fight."

"I'd fight too," she said, dragging herself away from her primary thoughts. "There's only so much the tribes will take. We're no better than the Boers, annexing Natal, then the Transvaal, just to show the Boers they can count on Imperial protection."

"You think there'll be a war?"

"If the Crown puts a poll tax on the Zulus, yes, I think they'll fight. Dinizulu's back from St. Helene, you know, and he'll do anything to keep his people from becoming gangs of cheap labor.

"David, I fear they'll take you," she added. She brushed my wind-blown hair away from my eyes. "You're seventeen, and being in the academy won't stop them."

Our bodies were covered with sea salt. I poured canteen water into a handkerchief, thinking to offer it to Maud first so that she could wipe her neck. But at the last second, I lifted her long hair out of the way and wiped the dry sea salt from the back of her warm neck myself. It was the most intimate gesture I had ever extended.

She loosened her collar. "That feels better," she said. "Here, give me the handkerchief, I'll do yours."

"It's all right," I said. "I don't want my collar wet."

"David, hold still. I won't wet your collar." She poured some canteen water into the handkerchief and rubbed the salt from the back of my neck and worked the wet handkerchief across my shoulders.

"There now, doesn't that feel better?"

We watched the fisher hawks leave the sky and dive into the sea and then bolt skyward with silvery fish locked in their hinged jaws. I lay back and wondered whether her affection—and her toleration of mine—could be called friendly, maternal, or something else entirely. The last thing I remember her saying was how she detested the coldness of London. How when she was in London she tried to make her flat as warm as Africa. She absolutely luxuriated in its tropical climate. Then I slept.

When I awoke I was alone. The air was rich with the pounding of the surf against the beach and the cry of the fisher hawks. I came down from the mossy boulder and called her name, then followed her footprints in the sand. The high-pitched voices of large swooping birds cried out all around me. Maud's footprints led me to a shady grove and I found her in a twilight green of orchids and ferns. She had been gathering coconuts and fruits from the low trees.

The sun had bleached her hair and I told her how fine she looked with her loose hair and her arms full of coconuts and fruits, and she said no one had ever said as much before.

My vacation was just about over, however, and I would soon be starting back for home.

The day before my departure, Maud and I lost ourselves in work. We were determined to gather all the tropical specimens that we could find and so spent the entire afternoon at a swamp pond about a mile from the Sanaga, two tired people with nets and specimen bottles.

It was truly an agonizing time for me. I tried to tell myself that my return home to Johannesburg was only a minor interruption of our time together, that nothing would really change. That in a short while we'd see each other again. That the world would stand still and we would remain forever after in each other's company.

In every Edenic garden there lurks the serpent, in every paradise there is the spoiler.

That very same day, when the sun had already caught the underside of the ferns and the orchids that hung from the lofty crowns of the mid-level trees, we were putting on our boots when Maud suddenly called out and fell against me. A scaly creature crawled into the underbrush.

Maud clung to me, pale and gasping, unable to rise. Blood trickled from a deep red spot on her ankle.

"Don't try to move," I said, and I placed a knapsack under her head. "Did you see it?" A bad feeling entered my chest.

She shook her head yes. I too had seen it. A scorpion.

"It burns," she said.

I worked fast. I tied a handkerchief around her ankle, which was already swollen with a ghastly blue shine, and opened my pen knife. She didn't say a word. We both knew what a scorpion bite meant.

Her brow was cold, her eyes turning glassy. Frogs began croaking and somewhere a snake hissed.

"I'm sorry, Maud," I said, "I've got to do this." Her face was twisted in pain and her breathing was forced. I pressed the penknife blade deep into the wound. Her mouth contorted in a single cry; then she went limp. I sucked out as much of the poison as I could. When I loosened the tourniquet, she regained consciousness.

"My legs. I can't move them," she said. Her pulse raced and her breathing pumped unevenly. The venom had attacked her nervous system. I prayed she wouldn't go into convulsions. I was very much aware that her life was in my hands.

Through the interlocking canopies a smoky darkness entered the forest and the lizards, the frogs, the carnivorous roaches stood poised as noisy beetles and crickets fled up mossy trees. Never before or since have I known such terror. Red termites ravaged fallen leaves and anything else that lay still for more than a moment. Giant butterflies cruised in the darkening air.

"I've got to get you back to the boat," I said. I knew I had a snake antidote in the medicine locker. She did not hear me. Had her breathing stopped altogether? I pressed my ear to her chest and heard the rapid beat of her heart. I tucked my trousers into my socks against the ants and raised her off the ground.

She lay heavily in my arms, and I could hear the fluids filling her lungs. Silky spiders and moths fluttered. Gossamer films masked my face. Swarms of mosquitoes went for my sweat. I called to her, but she was as alone in her darkness as I was in mine. I held her head against my chest, her legs dangling. Our hatchet marks on the tree barks were barely visible. Bats zigzagged erratically and legions of caterpillars crept up broad leaves.

In the thickening darkness I stumbled on roots and bumped into termite mounds and into man-sized succulents that bled when bruised, and gradually the shimmering trees ahead turned gray. Flowers faded and the shrubbery melted into watery hues and only a few pale grains of light held out against an encroaching night.

High above a monkey screamed, as if its skull had been crushed. I carried Maud in that owlish night, through warm, steamy vapors. The rising whir of insects replaced the bird sounds, and I pulled away from thorny vines that hooked me, caught me, and locked on me, until no matter which way I turned I was held by a thousand needles in a thickening jungle surrounded by the luminous green and yellow eyes of my tormentors.

I headed in what I thought was the general direction of the river, over fallen trees. The loud chatter of insects sounded in my ears like a jar of marbles spilled on a stony floor.

The darkness deepened into a more solid mass, and I soon lost the trail entirely. Now squads of yelling pygmy squirrels rushed overhead and I cursed the boldness of putrid-smelling monkeys that swung by on liana vines. From the intensity of their hysterical shrieks I knew an all-out attack was not out of the question.

My compass and lamp were in the launch and Maud's life was ebbing away. In anger, I drew Maud's revolver and fired blindly. There was a sudden stillness, then the rapid birth-scream of something large, followed by the coarse panic cry of a leopard-ravaged hog. I could smell the jungle's savage blood.

I pressed on, Maud heavier in my arms, her weight my weight, her breath my breath, her life my life. I had lost all track of time; I knew the moon was up there somewhere, but it belonged to another world beyond the jungle's blackness.

Then I heard the bellowing of elephants and could have sworn I saw a thundering herd charging with short turned-down tusks. Or did I only see a tree frog inches from my ear? Surah Am's talking spiders taunted me as I passed through their sticky webs.

"You're going the wrong way! You're lost! You'll never make it!" Their wiry voices vexed me. "Put her down, give up! Give up! Give up!"

"Bloody devils!" I cursed loudly.

I held Maud tightly and forged through the darkening screen of vegetation and tripped on low branches. I trudged onward blindly, unable to tell if I were moving or not, unable at times to feel my feet or my arms until I stumbled. I lost all track of time. Five minutes felt like an hour, ten minutes an eternity.

Beyond tired, beyond pain, a single thought drove me—to find the river. Backtracking, circling, shouting and praying, wandering in a daze and bitten by every species of insect in the forest, I fell to my knees several times, but somehow I kept Maud off the ground. I wanted to give up, but I didn't. I couldn't; I had to get her back to the boat. My neck was hot with fever, my arms bled from screw pine cuts. Exhausted, I stopped to rest.

I leaned against a tree with Maud cradled in my arms, not knowing in which direction to move. Trees that seemed close one minute were out of sight the next. I had reached the point of total fatigue, of total confusion. I could not take another step. Literally, I tried to move but could not. I had not the faintest idea in which direction to go, and without the benefit of that illusion, I could not move.

My bloody arms did not matter. It was my feet. I could not move them. They were stuck in a kind of mud. And Maud was slipping from my arms. I pulled one foot out of the mud and again the earth sank slowly under me; it was sandy and mucky, and as I lurched forward, Maud was suddenly light. I realized I was in water to my waist.

Up, beyond the jungle's canopy, was the broad sky deep in stars, and a high fang of a moon casting a pale glow on the Sanaga. And there, no more than twenty yards away from where I stood, cast in a dusty amber light, was the outlined form of the Land's End. Up to my hips in river mud, I hoisted poor Maud on board and then crawled up myself and lighted a lamp.

Her convulsions had subsided, but I dabbed the anti-neurotoxin around the open wound, which had since stopped bleeding, the pressure of my arms against her leg having acted as a tourniquet. Then I let a teaspoonful of the antidote trickle through her chattering teeth and lay her on her side. She had discharged mucous from her nose and mouth and I didn't want her to gag. Her feverish legs were not blue, a good sign. It was a question of her own inner resources riding out the effects of the poison. I covered her with an old raincoat.

Starting the engine, I threw on the bow beam and moved upriver. The somber moon lit up the parted waters of the Sanaga and soon, like the dark, rising walls of a serpentine canyon, the ebony forest on both sides of the river slipped by as the Land's End's flags whipped in the breeze, drowning out the drone of the passing jungle.

By the time we got back to camp, Maud's cramps had lessened and she could talk, but she was unable to walk very well. Surah Am had sent out searchers for us, and they had returned and were gathered outside his tent. I assured Surah Am that Maud would be all right and helped her toward her tent. Burning oil lamps surrounded the camp—a precaution against lions. The lamps, however dim, kept the big cats at bay.

I held Maud up while she washed herself, then I washed myself. Afterward, I put up tea while Maud lay on her cot. I was sorry to have taken so long to get her back. Her words broke through a tired smile:

"You were magnificent, Davey, and I shall never forget what you did." Then she added, sardonically. "Back home they'd say, had I died, 'What can you expect? She went to West Africa, the white man's graveyard.'"

"Try to keep your leg horizontal," I said. "You need a clean dressing." I feared gangrene. Her wound was red and her ankle still swollen. I cut a piece of linen—she had lots of it around—and got some antiseptic.

Despite her tiredness she said things she didn't want me to forget. "You understand, don't you Davey? Africa has given me all that I ever wanted…" Her breath was hard to come by, but her eyes fell on me directly. "And more," she said, "and more."

We could hear the cough of a lion circling our camp, and in the distant background, the grunts of a silverback gorilla. The other jungle sounds joined in, the crickets and cicadas, the beetles, the owls. But they no longer seemed a threat. A canvas tent, a pot of tea brewing on a stove, and a few oil lamps—they made the difference. I hesitated to place the antiseptic-doused bandage on her wound.

"Sting away," she said, bracing herself for the pain.

"Is that too strong for you?"

She reached for my hand. "I'll be fine, Davey, just fine."

But she was still badly shaken. The effects of the neurotoxin had unnerved her. She was also very tired. I held her hand and touched her forehead. She was never more beautiful. Even now, in the shadows of a hanging lantern, while a circling lion growled and apes roamed the Crystal Mountains' foothills, I saw a special beauty in her hollowed cheeks, her thin lips, her eyes partially hidden under a shank of damp hair. Her blouse barely covered her bony shoulders. Her fingers still held my own, keeping me near her.

I could not help myself. I brushed back the fallen hairs

from her eyes and brought her hand to my lips. The back of it grazed my brow. Then, feeling as if I'd somehow imposed myself on her, I rose quickly, went to the stove and brought two cups of tea. We drank in silence, slowly, watching each other. She had covered herself with a sheet and her skirt was on a basket beside her cot. When we finished the tea, I told her to sleep, that her fever was gone and I would see her in the morning. I drew her mosquito net. She seemed like a bride behind a veil. "Africa is my husband," I remembered she had told me.

Yes, I thought as I walked away, and I shall never be able to compete with such a husband. But then I heard her say my name. Her voice brought a stillness to my heart. My mouth was so dry I couldn't talk.

I turned and moved the netting to look at her. I saw in her eyes that she wanted me.

"Shall I remove my clothes?" I asked awkwardly.

She whispered yes and I removed them, blew out the lamp within reach and slipped in beside her and pulled the sheet over us. I heard the gentle flap of an owl's wing, the yearning of a jackal, the cicada's staccato chatter and the basso notes of the tree frogs.

I placed my arm around Maud's cool body and snuggled to her soft chest; she pressed her face against mine, and there in a tent in the rain forest, while the distant lanterns glowed, we lay together face to face, arm to arm. Outside our camp the circling lion growled unseen but heard and far back, before the mountains began, in the foothills where the low tree limbs stretched out in search of a higher light, the great apes roamed the forest looking for their mates.

It wasn't pleasure we sought that night as much as a certain completeness, a certain unbreakable truth. To have turned away from each other, for each of us to have gone back into ourselves, she to have gone off to sleep alone and I back to my own tent, would have been a lie.

Still, I could not be sure about her state of mind after all that had happened. Perhaps she had only meant to thank me for saving her life. Perhaps she needed to be loved to be certain that she was alive, that she would not succumb to the poison during the night and cease to be.

Thinking that she might find my presence at her side in the morning disconcerting, I rose early and returned to my tent before dawn. The brightening summer stars filled the sky beyond the crepuscular haze of our camp. There was the constellation Scorpius, a sprawl of sparklers just off the Milky Way, and its superstar, the ruby red Anatares, placed exactly where the celestial scorpion's heart should be.

We had breakfast together, as we always did, and once I ascertained that she was most definitely on the mend, I spoke of my return to my father's house in Johannesburg. I could tell she was not really listening, though she tried her best to look as though she were.

It was a bright day, and I thought to take one last look at Maud's museum collection; she had put everything in a special tent, a sort of laboratory that held her bottled specimens and plant samples. Winged specimens she kept alive in tanks and small cages. Everything was labeled and very impressive.

"Perhaps they'll name some of these things after you," I suggested. "Your name next to the Latin — Nux Volmica King."

She laughed. "If that happens, I'll insist your name be included."

"We were a good partnership," I dared to observe. There was so much to be said and so little time in which to say it. It suddenly seemed very important to me that one of us at least acknowledge that we had slept together. "You think Surah Am knows about last night?"

She nodded, then shrugged her shoulders.

I didn't want Surah Am and his workers talking about Ma. In fact, if it came out I was in her camp all summer it might hurt her someday—in Parliament perhaps.

"Are we ready?" she asked. She had offered to accompany me to the mail steamer station. There I would leave my launch and take a mail boat to Douala where I'd catch a southbound freighter. The sky was cloudless and bright, not a hint of rain—yet by two o'clock clouds would form, seemingly rising out of the steamy jungle, and it would rain for an hour or so.

"It's quite a trip to the station. Are you sure you want to go?"

"I'll take a dugout back. I'm sure." For a small coin any of the natives would be glad to row her back.

The sun caught Maud's golden hair in a wondrous way.

How I ever managed to tear myself away that day, I'll never know.

I shook hands all around, for I had come to know Maud's natives quite well by then, threw my knapsack in the launch and kicked over the old Daimler engine.

Maud got in the boat; she stood at the wheel with me; we waved at Surah Am and his men, then started down the river.

"I've enjoyed your company so much this past summer," she said.

"You'll see me again, Ma. After the new term starts, I'll be back."

"Who knows where I'll be by then, Davey. We are two small people in a very large world. Besides, the museum might grant me funds for an expedition."

"I'll find you," I said.

The river narrowed, and in the great silence between us we gazed at the lush rain forest, a profusion of apetalous flowers and long liana vines dangling from tall trees. Tribes of monkeys clamored on the high limbs, and we could hear the squawks of the macaws and the screams of the jays. This was the Africa she had given her life to, in order to explore its unknown rivers and mountains, its animals and plant life, its native customs and the unplumbed African personality. It was the Africa I was leaving for the civilized confines of home.

"You just take care of yourself," I said. "And stay away from scorpions."

She laughed. Her swelling had disappeared and she seemed perfectly normal.

"And you too take care. And write to me, even if the mail is three months late. I'll write you in care of the academy. I'm sure we'll make contact somehow."

When we reached the mail station, the steamer that would take me to Douala was waiting. I tossed my belongings on board and took a minute to put my launch in the postmaster's care. The steamer blew its first whistle. I got on board and stood at the rail. Standing at the dock's edge, Maud held my hand. We had never done that before, not even in private. I recoiled at the thought that I might not see her again, for what future could there be for me without Maud?

"I love you, Ma."

She smiled. I could see her eyes were watery, this strange, beautiful woman whom men had likely passed by in their rush for more run-of-the mill types.

The future was a blank, a shapeless hope. How I dreaded that the boat would move out and pull us apart. I held her hand tightly, as I would hold on to my own life.

The second whistle blew. "I want you to have this," she said, and she released her hand from mine to take from her pocket a small flannel purse. From it she extracted an ivory and gold ring, the one she had kept in her strong box, the one her father had given her.

"It's your father's ring," I protested. It shone brightly in the midday sun.

"I want you to have it." She smiled again, and as if apologizing, said, "It's just a token for all you've done." She placed it on the third finger of my left hand.

I felt extremely sad, for it seemed that such small things—as my father expecting me home in Johannesburg or Maud's expedition plans—it seemed these things, with no more substance than a mere thread, were able to prevail, and against the power of my unbreakable love. I couldn't understand it. But there it was. The third whistle blew.

I heard her last words from afar: "Goodbye Davey." She waved. And I stood there looking back at her until she became just a dot on the shore.

Chapter Five

My journey southward was long and tedious; the steamer's engine droned and I hardly ever slept. During the days I sank into a crocodile stupor. We'd put in occasionally at a coastal port and unload machinery and take on coffee and sometimes passengers. My life was empty without Maud.

One windy night, when the sea was high and I restlessly prowled the deck, I heard a familiar voice, a woman's voice. I made my way to the bow, but whoever had been there had already gone below. The next morning groups of well-dressed Europeans were lounging about the deck, but no one fit the voice I had heard. I decided that perhaps the wind had played tricks on me.

Several days later, however, as we neared Cape Cross on the southwest coast of Africa, with gulls overhead and the sea full of whitecaps, I heard that voice again. Not far from where I was, at the rail, stood a casually dressed man helping a woman focus the ship's telescope on a distant mountain, the Brandberg, I think it was. As I approached, my blood ran cold, for I realized the woman before me, whose red scarf flowed in the breeze, was the very woman whose voice I had heard on that windy night a few days before.

Adults don't change much in seven years. The same light hair, the same finely chiseled face. If it wasn't her, it was surely her reincarnation. My father had told me she had died in the bush. And though I had always suspected that she had run away, it was easier to live with the lie. Now that privilege would forever be behind me. She was at the ship's rail—with gulls overhead and a choppy sea full of whitecaps—my mother.

She avoided my stare and returned to the telescope. The chap with her, perhaps to cover her rudeness, asked me if I would like to look through the telescope. I said no.

"You're a South African, aren't you?" he said. His voice was brusque, a self-made man, I thought, on the short side, square shouldered, a handsome chap with thinning hair. "So am I," he added. "Cahill's the name. Roger Cahill. Jewelry's my line."

I shook his hand. "Unger," I said, "David Unger." He must have noticed how I studied his woman when I mentioned my name.

"Dearest," he said, "we've a compatriot on board. Mister David Unger. From around here, are you David? I know several Unger families in Queenstown."

"There's lots of us Ungers about," I said with a slight emphasis. The woman's eyes, just upturned slices of white under a heavy lash, barely met mine. I took her offered hand as if it were a piece of Dresden china. "Miss Rita Holland," said Cahill, and the woman put forth a brittle smile.

To think that she had carried me in that porcelain womb of hers. "My pleasure, Miss Holland."

Then turning to the gentleman, I added, "I'm from Johannesburg. I'm getting back from school."

Her embarrassment was nothing compared to the shame I felt. I couldn't bear to look at her. She surely must have sensed this. After more small talk, I nodded at Mister Cahill and continued my walk. Had I wished to, I probably could have encountered her again on the deck or in the lounge and pressed her to admit that she was my mother.

Instead, I went below. I had been lucky to get a cabin with a porthole, but now, my quarters seemed unbearably hot, dreary and cramped. Rows of rivets protruded from its wall and my clothes locker was so narrow I could only stick one arm inside at a time. An ancient desk and a rattan chair were under the porthole, my bunk against a vibrating wall adjacent to the engine room. These things had not bothered me before, but now they grated on my nerves. I felt feverish.

I tried opening the porthole, hinged with a metal cover, but the latch had been painted over and wouldn't budge. I felt as if I couldn't breathe. I took my shoe off and knocked the heel against the latch repeatedly, until my arm grew weary and I was sweating freely. Then, in total anger, I slammed the rattan chair against the porthole.

Of course, that did no good. In fact, one of the chair legs broke off.

I washed my face several times and rummaged through my duffel bag looking for I don't know what. That night I tried reading but couldn't concentrate. Every five minutes or so I heard footsteps on the deck above my ceiling, the heavy thuds of a man's and the sharp click of a woman's steps. Surely Roger Cahill and Miss Holland, like others on board, were promenading around the ship. I did not fall asleep until long after the footsteps stopped.

The next morning I brought the broken chair to the ship's carpenter, a sandy-haired fellow with a pointy nose and sharp-looking eyes; he wore a small leather apron. Attached to his walls were the tools of his trade.

"How did this happen?" he asked. Drunken brawls were quite common. His hair, his pointy nose and eyebrows were covered with sawdust.

"I don't know," I said, fearful of having to pay for the damage. "Perhaps it wasn't put together right. Things that aren't made right fall apart." I felt the sting of my own words. The carpenter took the chair and told me to come back the next day. He'd have it for me then.

I never went back. Something more important came up.

At the ship's next port of call, a group of Portuguese businessmen stunned us all with news that the Zulu nation was in open rebellion against the Crown; Dinizulu had attacked Imperial forces in the Transvaal.

By the time the ship reached Cape Town, Roger Cahill and his traveling companion had long since gone and while I was not glad that the war my father and Maud had predicted had started, I welcomed the distraction of such news.

The Cape Colony, it was called in those days, just a batch of islands, an inlet, then a sharp rise of land, a harbor, and the

Carolsburg castle at the entrance. The Zulu war was front page news when I got there; the hilly streets were packed with British officers in pith helmets riding around in rickshaws. Afrikaner Dutch was freely spoken and openly sharing the sidewalk traffic were Malay slaves, sheep farmers, and lots of traders, turbaned types, Indians mostly.

The feeling was that of a holiday despite the fact that Colony forces had already suffered casualties. White soldiers in soft pull-down hats crowded the saloons, a boisterous, swearing lot that stomped about in boots. On the broad avenues were marching bands.

On the darker side though, were the horse-driven lorries, jammed with prisoners; they too rattled over the cobblestones, dragging behind them long lines of blacks in chains, some still in warrior dress. They were on their way to the Carolsburg prison.

That afternoon I took a train directly to Johannesburg, a trip of over nine hundred miles. A noisy, eighteen-hour, chokingly dry, uneventful trip it was. When I got home my father greeted me at the door. He took measure of my size with his eyes, his gray hair cropped short and sticking out at the sides. He was dressed in a sleeveless shirt, his pants held up with suspenders. He had totally disowned his former self.

Nothing had changed in the house itself; still the same worn furnishings, smelling of the same old stale tobacco. The only difference was that the medical books were gone, sold probably. My father was fully installed as a worker, totally shorn of his former illusions.

"I told you, didn't I?" he said. I stood in the dark parlor, weary after a week of travel, a stranger in my own house. "Here, look at this." On the mantle was a letter from the war office.

He stuffed his pipe with tobacco, and cursing that it didn't draw well, he regarded me from the corner of his eye. He seemed to relish in the fact that the letter had caught me off guard.

A short sweet letter, it was right to the point. "In accordance with a declaration of war by the Zulu nation against the Province of Natal, you are hereby summoned by Her Majesty's command to report to the Ladysmith compound where you will be assigned to active duty for the duration of hostilities."

"But I'm still an academy student," I said. "I return to Craighill in September."

"You've turned seventeen, lad. Come September the entire Union may be overrun with Zulus. We lost twelve hundred at Isandlwana last time. That letter's been here a week already. You've been conscripted. Make no bones about it."

He drew on his pipe and regarded me with disdain.

At dinner that evening, I hit him with my own bomb. I told him that I had seen my mother.

"Aye," he said, raising his brow, "did you now? Back from the dead is she?" He looked at me long and hard, then decided I was telling the truth and relented a little. "And what did she have to say for herself, the proud banker's daughter, too good for the bloody likes of me?"

It was incredible how my father had adopted not only the

mannerisms but also the language of the laboring class.

"She said nothing about you. I only met her briefly. She regarded me a stranger and I preferred to remain so."

He watched me carefully behind a cloud of pipe smoke, perhaps sorry that I had to find out about my mother this way. "Just as well," he drawled. "She's become a regular Flying Dutchman, always on the run with never a home of her own." He let on that he would have preferred to tell me about her himself, but I never seemed quite old enough.

He said she had originally run off with a Hatlage chap, alias Harold Horn, alias Horace Huckabee. He had caught up with the chap once, but by then she had taken to another fellow, Spurlin, and after that, it was Bohler. He coughed a bit on his pipe smoke.

"It's Cahill now," I said, "Roger Cahill."

"Is that so?" He coughed several times more. When he looked up at me again, his eyes were watery. Then his face softened, and I understood, perhaps for the first time, that his anger toward me was tied to the fact that I was the son of the woman who had abandoned him.

He would have liked to talk to me about that abandonment, I think, and perhaps other matters as well, but we had to clear the table and then I had to get ready for Ladysmith. When I was young, he hadn't bothered with me, and now that I was a bit older, I had business of my own.

The next morning I was off to Ladysmith, not nearly as long a train ride as the agonizing journey from the Cameroon had been. At the start of the trip I fought against the idea that I might never see Maud King again. My meeting her had to have a purpose, a meaning. Our time together had to be more than just one fine summer. I thought of deserting, of taking the next train back to Johannesburg and returning to her. How could I have left her alone?

But we seldom live out our fantasies. And so through the dry country of grass tussocks and tufts of low trees and bushes the train whistled and the sun mercilessly beat through the window. Palm trees grew by the rivers, and there were lots of thorny trees elsewhere. Near the Newscastle station several women mourners wrapped in toboes were conducting a ritual, dancing and imprecating Maneh, their god, to allow them to find the missing soul of their dead brother. The conductor told me that from the looks of it, the man's soul couldn't be far. The man had been struck by a train the day before.

I pulled down the shade and traveled in semidarkness, a whole lot better than sweltering in the frying heat. Hours went by, and the sun refused to leave the sky. I now was glad I had been conscripted because even a week in my father's house would have been unbearable. The train rattled through the night; Ladysmith was waiting.

The Zulu war didn't last very long but it taught me a thing or two about so-called civilized people. By law, no British soldier could be ordered to touch a black. Now, that is something when you think of it. We, the British military, we could shoot the Zulus, these magnificent warriors, even hang them higher than a kite, but we could not be made to touch them. This, of course, turned into a shameful situation for the Zulu battlefield wounded, for unless there was someone to hoist them onto a stretcher, and then put them in an ambulance and transport them to the Ladysmith hospital, they would die where they had fallen, by the thousands.

Luckily, though, one man assumed the responsibility, a small, skinny, bespectacled Indian sergeant major, an ambulance driver. We called him Bapu. He commanded a gang of twenty-four Indian stretcher bearers—although that number hardly sufficed against the mounting Zulu casualties. When I learned he needed another driver, I volunteered.

Bapu, in his private life, I soon learned, practiced law in Johannesburg. Many of his clients were poor and beaten in spirit. With them he worked for free; the money people he charged. He was concerned with the mechanics of power. I remember one time a beautiful woman boarded a bus we were on. Every man on the bus stopped talking and looked at her. Bapu turned to me and said, "There is a lesson in this. See how beauty commands silence, how men are transformed, raised above themselves? Beauty has a power to raise us from a common fate, as prayer does. But it brings on its own destruction, beauty does. A barbarous nation gains power through the destruction of another nation's enchantments, its gods, its chance for a better life. I am speaking symbolically, of course."

"No," I said, "you are speaking of Britain in India, Britain in South Africa."

He didn't immediately respond. "What I'm saying is that beauty is one source of power. There are others. Force and prayer for instance."

Bapu had a modest farm in the Durban area, and on weekends I went there and spent time among his friends. I wrote Maud a letter from the farm and addressed it to the Sanaga River station. I told her I had been conscripted and was in the Natal Ambulance Corps and that I drove to and from the front each day.

Meanwhile the Zulu war continued into the hot summer, intense but sporadic, a series of tribal raids and Imperial counterattacks. Dinizulu couldn't be persuaded to reach an accord.

One time toward evening, before the others gathered, Bapu told me he had decided to renounce the material world's enchantments.

"He who would seek a new world for his people must seek nothing for himself." He said that all work was equal, and that although anger was a power and vital in the war against colonial oppression, it was only through the renunciation of the self, the subversion of an inner hostility, that one could attain a truly spiritual state. Weapons, he said, were incapable of total victory; having them only strengthened the enemy.

"If you would subdue your foe, bring him to your side. A friend is weak against a friend," he told me. And he went on to speak of the power of goodness, of purging oneself, of making oneself as malice-free as a tree. He felt this power easily extended to the animal kingdom as well.

I was skeptical. But he was willing to show me what he meant. The sun had just fallen across the expanse of his farm and birds crossed a field to a nearby orchard. I watched, quiet and amazed, as he placed himself in a trance. His face became expressionless; his demeanor betrayed no thought, no trace of intelligence. He truly resembled a thin tree.

While I looked on, he walked to the field, and there he stood, hip high in swaying grain, his arms outstretched, lifted slightly upward, while birds flew past him. Then, as I watched, some of the birds began to hover near him. They circled closer and closer to his outstretched arms. And finally, one bird perched on his arm. Then another. And soon both his arms held the weight of many birds.

When he returned to where I was, he said, "It is only the malice of man the birds fear. But a tree is neutral." His smile was barely discernible. "So if you would pass a wild beast unharmed, make yourself as a tree. Concentrate, purge yourself of all malice and when a coldness enters your arms and legs, you will know you have succeeded."

Later that evening under the vines of his front yard he told his friends and family that he had decided to abandon his law practice and devote his life to serving humanity. He took two oaths that night: celibacy and poverty. "He who would seek a new world for his people must seek nothing for himself," he said again.

The meeting that night reminded me of the one presided over by Cecil Rhodes at my father's house. Rhodes, too, had embarked on a mission, the carving of an empire from the jungles north of the Transvaal for the greater glory of Britain. Rhodes had employed wealthy men to become even wealthier. But this was not nearly as grand a mission as the one Bapu was undertaking, the transformation of himself, the subordination of his instincts to the interests of a principle, the renunciation of material wealth.

Bapu: Later the world would know him as Mahatma Gandhi.

There are times when nothing seems to go right. In the middle of a letter, your pen runs dry and you can't find your ink bottle; your pencil breaks. The lamp oil can won't unscrew. You hang out some clothes to dry, the wind shifts, and the clothes end up covered with soot. One summer morning it was just like that for me. A run of bad luck? Jinxed? It doesn't matter what you call it, but that particular morning there was no letting up, and I ended up more than just cursing mad.

The night before I had gotten word that the Nongoma Valley had been overrun by Natal forces, so at daybreak I drove my ambulance into that region's wilderness, a beautiful place filled with the purple flowers of jacaranda trees. As soon as I arrived my bearers jumped out of the truck and went looking for the wounded. I don't know exactly what I was doing, just walking in circles in a distracted kind of way. Perhaps I was scanning the sky for buzzards, for they always gave you a clue as to where the suffering bodies were. A battle had taken place not far from where I had parked. There were bullet holes in the trees, and Zulu artifacts were scattered every-where—armbands, breastplates, leather pouches. Then I realized I had lost my ignition key. I frantically searched the ground. Finally I found the key, only to discover that my front tire was flat. I had driven over a broken spear.

That was it. I raised a storm. I kicked and cursed the ambulance. Finally I got down to changing the tire. Out came the jack; up went the ambulance; off came the wheel; on went the spare. It didn't occur to me that I hadn't seen my bearers in over an hour. Not a peep from any of them.

I was just finishing with the tire when I noted the greenery parting. Beyond the foliage, a band of Zulu warriors, with headdresses of lion manes and with their torsos covered with beaded shields, watched me from a short distance. Silently, they drew closer. Then, with grunts and growls, they took turns jabbing me with spears and nothing I said (I spoke a Xhosti dialect of Bantu, which was the common language in the north) convinced them I was there on their behalf.

They took me to the mountainside, tied a bush rope around my waist, and despite my continuing protestations, pushed me down a dark narrow opening, an oubliette, a womb-like passage in the grotto floor that descended into the bowels of the earth. Down I went, my pleas unheeded, through a crevice barely wider than my shoulders into a suf-focating heat.

I choked on the dry, limestone dust and was trying to climb back up when suddenly my legs were dangling free, the air was breezy beneath me and I was surrounded by soft, plaintive cries. I was under the canopied ceiling of a spacious cavern. And bats, all sizes, with their flapping, ribbed, leathery wings and mice-like cries, darted by me, undaunted, but attracted all the more, it seemed, by my swinging legs. Choking, hollering, I was lowered even deeper, until my view of the sky retreated and with it the sounds of the outside world. In silent darkness now I descended, and the only sound I heard was that of the bats and my own labored breathing.

I clung to the rope. I dropped in jerks, two or three feet at a time, the extension of a man's arm length. The rope worked its way through the loose earth and down came rocks and dirt. I threw out my legs to swing out of the way of the falling rocks and hoped to catch a ledge, a crevice, anything that might arrest my fall. By now my swings were fairly wide but still I was lowered. I continued to choke on the dust. Then, beyond my coughing I detected the familiar sound of English voices.

Finally I touched down. I managed to get myself out of the rope. It was jerked from my hands before I could even wonder what would become of it. I looked about myself; I was surrounded by about fifty heavily-bearded British soldiers. Prisoners, just as I was.

"'Ave yourself a drink, lad," a soldier said. And I was handed a canteen.

It took me a while to get my bearings. The prisoners were badly undernourished and so weak they could barely walk. Luckily, though, they had water. As for food, I learned soon enough, they subsisted on frogs and bats. Many had already died. The strong ones, they claimed, were culled out from time to time and sent to a nearby Zulu gold mine.

The cave was large, maybe twenty square acres. Against its far wall was a dark pool, a pond, actually, that was replenished by water that continually dripped down the wall. The pond was filled with frogs and other crawling things. At the cave's mouth, which was at the end of an incline, two chained lions stood guard, a male and a female. The men called them Punch and Judy.

The Zulus had stationed them there with makeshift collars, two snarling beasts, straining at their chains. If you ask me, their anxiety wasn't so much about their loss of their freedom as it was the frustration they must have felt being unable to reach us and satisfy their carnivorous hunger. The chains let them enter about ten feet into the cave—just enough to keep anyone from rushing past them.

That was the situation. Two of our officers, I was told, had tried to escape, the last one by bashing his way out with a rock in each hand. But he got no farther than the first officer, who had tried sprinting past the lions. Both had had their bones picked clean.

I soon got used to the fact I was a Zulu prisoner. From time to time there would be an unholy roar at the mouth of the cave as a tribesman would come by to throw some raw meat before the lions and bring them buckets of water. Our own drinking water came from that canteen that we passed around. We took turns filling it by pressing it against the wall and letting water trickle into it. It was a very time-consuming procedure but a necessary one, for the water in the pond was useless. We could use it only to bathe.

I ate my share of frogs, though I drew a line at eating bats. I exercised and refreshed myself the same as the other prisoners did, by swimming in the dark pool. At night, I gathered with the others and watched Corporal Wimpenny.

George Wimpenny was a professional entertainer, a regular song and dance man. He had played the main clubs in South Africa. Each evening before retiring, he'd put on a show—saloon ditties, impersonations, that sort of thing. And sometimes he'd thrill us with his magic. He was a tall string bean with a shock of bushy hair, a bony face and a protruding Adam's apple. His job was to keep our spirits up. He borrowed our rings and made them disappear before our very eyes. His expertise with a deck of cards was truly baffling. He restored a cut piece of string. (Later he told me the trick is "don't cut the string to begin with.") And the oldest trick of all, cups and balls. Under which cup was the pebble? Here, there, where? Why everywhere and nowhere. He moved the pebble invisibly to our utter astonishment.

Without him, most of the men would have perished. At first I was in no mood for his entertainments; I preferred to brood over the absence of Maud King from my miserable life. But eventually I fell in with Wimpenny's antics. We became friends, in fact, and he taught me a few basic moves.

And I in turn taught him—or at least explained to him— some of what I had learned from Gandhi. He was a willing student. For hours on end, we talked about purging the body of hostility, subduing the senses to zero. At his request, I told him over and over again the story of how the little Indian had transformed himself from a man like any other into a tree.

One night I got up and there was Wimpenny near the mouth of the cave, his chin resting on his folded arms bridged across his knees, gazing at the lions. I stared with him for a time, then asked, "Are you thinking the same thing I am?"

He smiled. "I wouldn't try it. These lions have already tasted human blood."

Wimpenny was right, of course. But the men were slowly dying. The lions' long bodies lay across the cave's entrance. I crawled closer to the male. His dusty ears perked and his tail moved. I slowly put out my hand to allow him to smell me. A human smell. He snarled softly, warning me to keep my distance. I inched closer. He snarled louder this time, showing his teeth, and the female behind him stirred too. I withdrew.

"Forget it, it's no go," whispered Wimpenny. "He sees you as a potential meal. Better go back to sleep. I'd rather end up in a gold mine."

I studied the lion. If only he could get used to me. A friend is weak against a friend, Bapu once said. I went back to my foxhole and Wimpenny eventually went back to his. But instead of sleeping I thought of what Bapu had said about entering a neutral state, of ridding oneself of human malice.

Just before dawn I awoke, and as if I had been rehearsing all through my sleep, I went immediately to sit near the mouth of the cave, about a foot away from the male lion's farthest reach. The huge beast breathed rapidly. I could feel his body's heat and I could swear I heard the pounding of his heart and smelled the limestone he rolled in.

I concentrated on purging myself of malice. For what seemed like many hours, I recalled every wrong done to me and forgave them each in turn. I forgave my mother for abandoning me and my father's anger. Truly and fully I forgave them. Then I forgave myself for all of the wrongs I had inflicted, and I was surprised at how many I was able to recall. I felt I was wringing out every vestige of malice from my heart, as if it were a rag, until there wasn't a drop of malice left in me.

For a long time thereafter I fixed my eyes in a stony stare and attempted to empty myself of thought as well. At first the task seemed impossible, but gradually I became aware of a flute-like sound, a music, a dim vibration seemingly in the very air I breathed. The music grew more distinct. My vision, meanwhile, seemed to grow dimmer. Then it seemed as if the visible world lost its edge entirely and the lions and the rock wall melded into a single opaque, cloudy image. A chill entered my bones.

I felt lighter, as if my blood had drained from my limbs and my humanity had oozed out of me. The clothes I wore clung strangely to my skin, and as the music, the vibration, grew clearer and the chill in my bones more pronounced, a darkness fell over my eyes and I longed for the warmth of the sun.

My heart barely beat, and my hands and my face felt as implacable as stone. I sat there suspended between sleep and wakefulness, in a dream-state, a trance. I had become as neutral as a tree. Bapu had held his trance while he had walked out to a field. I only had to move forward a bit.

On my hands and knees I entered the male lion's orbit. He hardly stirred. His great heart had calmed. He was breathing normally, although I was well within his grasp. I slowly rose to my feet and stepped to the lion's side. The great cat's yellow eyes half opened and he pressed his maned head against my leg and from deep in his throat came a tremulous purr. Behind him the lioness stretched her front legs forward and hunched her back. I carefully removed the lion's collar and then the lioness' too. Their chains eased to the ground. I walked out of the cave. It was still dark, but the lions followed. They sniffed the air and then freely trotted across the rocky slope to meet the dawn that was on its way.

I sat on a rock and watched them disappear. I could feel my humanity returning. Although the sun would not rise for a while yet, I felt warmth return to my limbs. Then I went to Wimpenny and woke him up. "The lions have gone. I've freed them," I said.

"You what?" He bolted upright and stared toward the mouth of the cave. The first thin tree lines of the new dawn allowed him to see that the lions were truly gone.

"By Jove!" he declared. "Where are they?" He rubbed his eyes. "I don't believe it! They are gone!" He got up suddenly and ran out of the cave and then back in. He flung his fists in the air and shouted at the top of his lungs for the men to get up. Get up! Get up! They were free!

A wild time we had of it that morning, with the cheering and celebrating; the men threw caution to the wind entirely.

They had, everyone one of them, given up of ever coming out of the cave alive. They even tried carrying me on their shoulders, they were so grateful. But as the old saying goes, the spirit was willing but the bodies were weak. They hadn't an ounce of strength left in them. As it was, we had to walk a good distance to the road where I had entered the valley in my ambulance. We knew we could flag down any lorry passing through, and we did.

At Ladysmith we learned that Dinizulu had been captured and that the war had been over for a week. In the eleven days that I was in the cave I had seen three men die. Had we stayed in the cave any longer, the number would have been much higher. We learned that the soldiers who had worked in the gold mines had not fared any better. In fact, their mortality rate was even greater than ours. After a week at Ladysmith, Wimpenny and the rest of the men were given a month's furlough. I was still with the academy, of course, still a student. So I was discharged.

Chapter Six

My senior year at the academy was torture. I saw nothing of Maud and couldn't contact her. My first letter to her in care of the Sanaga postal station went unanswered, so did the others I sent throughout the year to the British Museum, on the off-chance that she was still dealing with them. I had no way of knowing the British Museum had already underwritten her expedition and that she was gone.

All I knew was that I'd cross the bay each Saturday as usual and Ma, the woman trader, the friend and benefactor of the Sanaga River tribes, was not at any of the villages. One week I took the Land's End as far east as Tibati. I even approached a tribe of pygmies in the vicinity, not far from the Adamaoua Mountains. But no one had seen Maud. She had totally disappeared.

Finally it occurred to me to contact the museum directly and inquire if they knew of her whereabouts, and that's when I learned they had commissioned her to explore the entire West Africa region. But no, they had no idea of exactly where she was. If I wished to see her, I had to wait until she returned to England.

I waited. I spent a good deal of time practicing tricks that

I had learned from Corporal Wimpenny in the cave. Magic had become of great interest to me, and attempting to practice it perfectly helped the time to pass.

England, of course, was another world. Maud and I were both in Africa, but still a continent apart.

One day I received a letter postmarked Smythesburg, in Orange River Colony. Our local pastor back home wrote that my father had passed away in his sleep and his burial had been arranged from a public fund.

I was jolted by the news. First I felt anger, then a sense of betrayal set in, and finally the sad knowledge that the tension between my father and me had never been resolved. We had not gotten along, but even in the most antagonistic situations there exists the secret hope that things will somehow turn around in the end. Death, though, is very final.

Back to Smythesburg I went, a lonely journey. A tramp steamer dropped me off at Cape Town and I rode through a sleepless night in a third-class coach rattling into the shadeless glare of dawn. By the time I reached Smythesburg my emotions were burned out of me and I felt empty inside.

My father had found his final peace in a fenced cemetery that overlooked the Vaal river. Under the willows and the Kalahari thorn trees, the Reverend Carmichael read from a psalm:

And he shall be like a tree planted by the river
That brings forth his fruit in its season; and his leaf
Shall not wither and he shall prosper.

My father had not prospered in this world. Maybe in the

next world he would and in that regard I wished him luck. I stayed in Smythesburg just long enough to put his house on the market and dispose of his few possessions. One of his things I kept, an old linen jacket in which I found a thin volume of Marcus Aurelis' *Meditations* inscribed by his old friend Cecil Rhodes. Everything else went to charity.

Eventually I found myself in London, at King's College on a scholarship, studying, among other things, courses that would prepare me to study medicine. In those days a scholarship meant tuition money, nothing more. So money was still scarce as far as general expenses went. But thanks to Corporal Wimpenny, I had a large assortment of tricks now, and on weekends I entertained as a magician in the London clubs; in that way I got by.

For the most part, though, I went from the classroom to my flat; my life was stale, to say the least. Here and there I established friendships, a few of them with women my age, but none was of any consequence. The magic shows were my only real diversion.

Time passed. Some days my recollection of Maud felt as thin as the recollection of a long ago dream. I could not remember what she looked like or the sound of her laughter. And when that happened I feared that one day I would lose her altogether, that I would be left with a nameless emptiness in my heart. But then there would be moments of clarity, when I could see her face and hear her voice as plainly as if she were at my side.

One day when I was in my junior year, I was sitting on a park bench wondering what I might do with my life when a discarded newspaper caught my eye. The headline read: BRITISH WOMAN EXPLORER SCALES WEST AFRICA'S HIGHEST PEAK.

I raced to pick it up before the wind could carry it away. Amazingly, the story introduced Maud King, a "traveler, explorer and a scion of a renowned family." I read and learned that Maud had been the first white woman to climb West Africa's highest mountain (not for glory, but to discern the direction of another mountain range), and that she also had traversed the deadly Ogowe River rapids for hundreds of miles.

I recalled a time she had run a broken fingernail across a map of Gabon and said, "This is where I plan to go." Now she had gone to that very place, and done more than that, much more.

The press had discovered her. I read every word the *Times* and the *Daily Telegraph* printed about her. They compared her to Mungo Park, Sir Richard Burton and Speke.

Knowing where Maud was, however, was worse somehow than not knowing, because I knew too the danger of what she was doing. And the fact that Surah Am was at her side was not much consolation.

Later newspaper reports told of her encounter with cannibals in the uncharted regions of the Lower Congo. Some sensational magazines even said that she had made herself a queen among the Congo cannibals. Other stories asserted that she was preaching nationalism to the West African tribes and the museum would rue the day it had commissioned her work.

I continued with school, of course, and my weekend club work. For me it was a period of longing and uncertainty. I wondered if this adventurous woman explorer, who had captivated the press with her exploits, still remembered the young cadet who had delivered her mail when she had traded on the Sanaga—the same cadet who still wore the ivory and gold ring she had placed on his finger.

The answer to that question came one rainy Friday in November of my senior year. The entire week before that fateful day the newspapers had hailed the return to England of the African explorer, the great heroine Maud King. Every day in the newspapers and magazines she was quoted—and misquoted too, I'm sure. One day she was praised, the next day embroiled in controversy. On the one side she was attacked by racists, and on the other side hailed as the New Woman.

I thought of calling on her, but it seemed the minute she touched British soil she embarked on a lecture tour organized by the publisher of a book she had just written. I followed her excursions to Edinburgh, Glasgow, Birkenhead, Liverpool, Vauxhall and Ireland. Then I read that she was returning to London from Dublin.

Her return would have been hard to miss. The day before she was due back, there were men wearing sandwich boards, strutting up and down Oxford Street as human advertisements of Maud's upcoming London lecture. For ten guineas you could see, hear and share a cup of tea with the great Maud King. It was all very intimidating.

The morning of the day that she was to meet with Parliament was overcast; later it began to rain. Looking out of my classroom window, I said to myself, Well, Davey, here is the opportunity you've been waiting for. All you need to do is ride over to the House of Commons. That's where she'll be. But it was raining, and I had left my umbrella at home.

Of course that wasn't the real reason I hesitated. So much had happened—to her at least—since I had seen her last. Why should she even remember me? And she was famous now. I resigned to step back into the shadows of her past.

That afternoon, after my last class, I descended the stairs to the spacious main lobby of the university building, my books under one arm, a raincoat under the other. In the crowded lobby bantering students opened and closed doors and unfurled umbrellas. The marble floor was wet and slippery. From the half-open auditorium door I could hear the school orchestra practicing inside. I listened, hoping to kill some time until the rain let up. Meanwhile, students kept filing through the lobby, whipping off their raincoats and shaking out their umbrellas.

Then a glimpse—a hatless, light-haired woman in a raincoat near the giant double doors; that's all I saw, maybe a leather shoulder strap and a briefcase, a slender figure, nothing more. The woman could have been a teacher, a visitor, anyone. The opening and closing doors prevented my getting a better look. It was sheer chance, anyway, that I was in the hallway at that very moment. I could just as easily have decided to leave the school early or by another exit. The notion that I might easily have been elsewhere allowed me to dare to hope; my heart beat rapidly. Could it be? Was I hallucinating? My legs were weakening. I had no right to expect as much. I went toward her, bracing myself against a gross disappointment.

The loudspeakers announced class changes. Bedlam erupted—with the noise, the umbrellas, the books, the coats everywhere, with half the damn school trying to empty out and the other half trying to get in. A human tide of arms seemed an insurmountable barrier. I lost ground in the congestion and was carried away from her. I needed a better look, but I couldn't move forward. The bodies in raincoats seemed a solid separating wall. In total exasperation, I called out. "Maud! Maud!"

The woman turned ever so slightly; she turned as a bird might, as a bird in an aviary might tilt its head in recognition of a kindred call amidst the chaotic, cacophonous uproar of alien songs. That's all she did, just tilted her head. But that slight tilt was enough to assure me that she had recognized my voice. And the straining glimpse I had of her kept alive the possibility. Then she turned fully and I saw her. Maud King.

Her look was one of both perplexity and joy. That's the look she had that day in the hallway at King's College. She had heard me but she didn't see me. I called out again. "Maud! Maud! Here!" The blood in my veins sang with joy.

She called back with tears of gladness. My throat tightened; my heart cracked, and although buffeted, bounced, elbowed and kneed, we neared each other. I remember the moment our fingers touched, how we entwined them and held tightly against the human tide.

In spite of the commotion, I forgot where I was—where we were. For a moment at least I was transported back to the Sanaga, to the jungle, to the reed huts and the ceremonial dances, to the long nights we had spent together listening to music on the gramophone, to the time on the beach when the fisher hawks dove into the sea. I remembered the night ride up the Sanaga after the scorpion had bitten her ankle, the night we returned to camp and made love—a boy of seventeen and a full-grown woman, perhaps with just as little experience. I remembered our parting, when she put her father's ring on my finger.

We found a corner away from the tumultuous mass. I had expected to awaken at any moment and find I'd been dreaming. But no, Maud and I were together. "God, Davey," she said, "you're such a handsome sight. Just look at you!"

I had a beard; I wasn't a young cadet anymore.

"Thank God,'" she cried, with tears brilliantly filling her eyes. "I gave it one last desperate try just this morning. And here you are. I called the school and they said you were registered. I couldn't believe it. I had thought…"

"I thought you'd forgotten me," I said when she paused. "Your expedition's been in all the papers. I tried so long to track you down." She seemed not to have aged: The same blue eyes, the shallow cheeks, the broad forehead.

"God of Mercy, David, you don't know! The museum just handed me your letters this morning. I've been on a lecture tour, and it seems someone decided I would prefer to have my mail saved until my return." She dug into her briefcase. "They'd been holding them for years, it seems. The idiots! One's post marked three years ago. Here, look."

I kept my hand on her shoulder. I didn't want to let her go, not even for a minute. "That's the one I sent you telling you I'd been captured but escaped."

"And this second letter, postmarked just a month later…"

"Yes, when they told me I'd been discharged from the Natal forces."

"It's been such a terrible mess, Davey, such an awful needless worry."

"You thought I was dead. Of course you did. What else could you think?" I felt at fault myself. "After a while I stopped writing. I knew I wasn't connecting. I even thought that maybe you preferred it that way."

"You thought that?" She seemed genuinely surprised.

"There could have been someone. There might still be. I don't know."

She smiled deeply and tilted her head so that it touched my shoulder for just a moment. "Oh God, Davey, it's so good, our being together again." Her smile broke into laughter.

I dropped my eyes and didn't know what to say. Students' elbows found us even in our corner.

"The War Office said you were missing in action." Our eyes

met again. "Your letter, it said you were a prisoner for eleven days. Then why...? What I can't understand is why in God's name was I told you were still out there. In the war zone. Why?"

"They had undoubtedly forgotten to update their lists, their damn missing-in-action lists."

She nodded in agreement. "The nincompoops. All they're good at is killing. But thank God, David, you're alive. I can't get over the way you look." Her hand touched the roughness of my face. "You're alive."

From the auditorium came the sound of Beethoven's *Ode to Joy*. For a moment we listened. We had played that record so many times during our Sanaga days. Then we left the building and danced down the stone steps into the rain.

At a tea shop she explained that the only letter she had gotten from me was the one that mentioned that I had been conscripted.

"And that's how you learned I'd been missing in action."

"I asked the War Office at what battle site you'd been to. The fools wouldn't tell me. I was not your wife, they said, nor your sister, nor your mother. But I was persistent and one of them finally let on. The Nogoma Valley, he said."

"Oh Maud, no."

"I searched the area. And I'd have searched ten more like it. Only they forced me to leave. They said the fields were under quarantine. They lied. There was no such thing."

"So you went off to the Congo thinking I was dead."

"What else was I to think? Then the museum expedition

proposal came through. I'd have explored Hades had they asked me to. This morning when I read your letters…in your last one you said you were going to King's College. I immediately called the admissions office."

"And here you are."

We silently left the tea shop. I went over our conversation in my mind. It seemed to me that her actions had been—and her words were—those of a woman in love; but I couldn't be certain, and I couldn't bring myself to ask for fear of learning that I was wrong. The tropical sun had given her skin a rose tone, and it set off her light hair; her eyes too had an uncommon radiance. There was so much to talk about. She said she had some business in Kent. Could I spend the weekend with her at Crossgate, her home? I had no proper clothes, I said, but if we stopped off at my flat, I might pick up a few changes. Which is just what we did.

Then off to Charing Cross we went and took the next train south. As we sped through the countryside, she told me the museum wanted her to make another expedition to West Africa, to the upper Congo this time.

"You're not giving it serious consideration, are you?" I was quite disturbed.

She needed time to think it over. We rode in silence for a while, each of us gazing at the other, then returning to our own thoughts. The idea of her returning to Africa had taken the edge off my new-found bliss. But then again, I thought, why should I not have the power to sway her? In the jungle I had always gone to her. This time she had come to me.

We arrived at Crossgate in the silvery dusk, shivering and damp, with our arms full of groceries. There's nothing quite like an English rain. It's like a breathable powder. It permeates the air rather than washes through it.

Maud's cousin, Rita Anthony King, the one who wrote children's books, normally used the house, but she had taken a long holiday on the Continent, and so we had the place to ourselves. The house was a handsome two-level seventeenth century Tudor, with gables protruding from a high attic. It stood far back from the road and was framed among mature trees that allowed for a formal garden out front, however neglected it appeared.

There were trellised vineyards in the back and flower gardens separated by a stony footpath that led to a gazebo. Under a willow stood a stooped tool shed. Farther back was an apple orchard. Its gnarled trees appeared posed as if props in a macabre ballet. To think that this same Maud, for whom I'd once bought a hat because she didn't have a decent change of clothes, could have grown up here.

Once inside the drafty and dank house we opened the shutters and the remaining dusty light seeped into an oak-paneled great room. Portraits of the King family, which hung on the walls, were barely discernible in the dark room. Her father's people were of the disenfranchised gentry class—which meant lots of titles but no money. The more successful ended up as bishops or in the military, and the black sheep ended up in the tropics.

"So you see my African journey was no accident," Maud

said jokingly.

We lit a fire in the massive Jacobean fireplace and the dancing flames quickly drove out the cold and the dampness. That done, Maud wound and set the grandfather clock in the hall. For Maud, the house was a tax liability, but she couldn't bring herself to put it on the market; it had been in the family for too long. Besides, Rita Anthony took good care of it.

In Maud's bedroom, the sanctuary of her childhood and adolescence, stood a four-poster bed and shelves of books. The walls were papered in a floral pattern. Everything was neat and in place, just as Maud had left it before her African years. On a table by the mullioned windows was a microscope under a flannel hood. Her room was so different than my own back home. A book was left open on her night table and I read a small poem, which ended:

> Creep home, and take your place there,
> The spent and maimed among:
> God grant you find one place there,
> You loved when all was young.

"Perhaps someday you'll come back to all this," I urged. "Creep home and take your place..."

"I don't think so," she replied, fixing her hair in her mirror. "My real home is elsewhere now." She went to the window and looked down on the yard. "I need to be free, David. I thought you knew that."

I knew exactly what she meant. She was, in some sense, defining our relationship as well as the one she had with Africa. Her words stung. "Free? Free from what?" I asked, and

I felt in that moment less like the man she had returned to than the boy she had known.

"You must be hungry, David," she said. "Let's make ourselves some dinner. You're going to love our stove."

I stopped her on the stairs, my hand on her arm. "Free from what?"

She fixed me firmly in her gaze. "From being a woman, of course."

I let go of her, even more perplexed than before.

That evening we cooked on the great stove in the kitchen and the house grew warmer still. Maud luxuriated in warmth. She kept the downstairs as close to tropical temperatures as possible. We ended our meal with a glass of wine, then, when the night chill came, we sat on the rug before the fireplace with our knees in our arms. I told her about Bapu and Wimpenny and my eleven days as a Zulu prisoner. I even mentioned that I had run into my mother. Maud's doings were public knowledge, of course, but I was anxious for the details of her activities. During the course of our conversation, she mentioned that she had been asked out to dinner by a bureaucratic administrator in the Colonial Office, who, she said, was probably interested in advancing his career. She was at a bit of a loss as to how to deal with him.

"And what if he's genuinely interested in you and only you?" I asked.

"Davey, please. He lives with his mother and he wears a hothouse orchid in his lapel." We both laughed.

We drew closer to each other and before long, while the fire blazed and our faces grew warmer, a tiredness came over us and we slept in each other's arms under an afghan that her father had once brought home from one of his travels. When the grandfather clock struck three, I awoke and carried Maud up to her room and put her in bed. I slept in a nearby chair.

The next morning Maud dressed in a casual manner. She had very little to wear, actually. Most of her clothes, she said, had a closet odor. We walked into the town of Mayfair. She wanted to show me her childhood haunts. The drizzle was so fine that we didn't need to open our umbrellas. Then Maud stopped off to have some papers notarized at a pharmacy and I noticed a poster in the window. The Art Society and the Philanthropic something or other were co-sponsoring a social evening at the Kensington Hall. Maud King was named as the guest of honor.

"Maud," I said, "they've got you listed as the big pot."

She begged me not to remind her.

After I'd seen her ivy-covered grammar school, we walked along the Rather River. There was a quietness that hung over Kent like a heavy fog. It was as if something had been put to rest centuries ago and nothing dared disturb it, not the sheep in the soft meadows or the low horn of the boats on the river, and certainly not the drizzling rain.

We visited a solemn, ancient church, St. Cyr's, and while we wandered among the aged tombstones, Maud approached the vicar, a silver-haired gent, who was getting an estimate for some repairs to be done on the church's stonework. She shook his hand and spoke to him briefly, as she would an old family friend.

We left the church and walked under a line of tall oaks at the side of the road. I could not help but feel left out that she had not introduced me to the vicar. But I couldn't blame her for not wanting the townspeople to know I was staying at her house. I asked if she had reached a decision on her upper Congo expedition—the one the museum wanted her to make.

She had not. Then after a pause, she said, "It would be poor form, David, to refuse. They did finance me, after all."

"You owe them nothing," I argued. "You've tripled their donations with all the publicity you've gotten."

"This English sky," she responded, "just look at it. It makes me nervous, full of small, flitting sparrows, its thin clouds that constantly drizzle. Really, I feel more at home in Africa, more needed, more my own self. There's so much that needs doing there. Besides, I have a duty toward the tribes, a small but simple duty in exchange for what they have given me."

"But you've done more than your share already. Maud, can't you see, you've allowed this so-called duty to run your life."

"David, know one thing. You are a very real part of me. That's the truth. And whatever I do for the tribes now it will be because I can share something in me that you have put there."

"Be that as it may, all I'm trying to say is first you had a duty to your family that you had to consider, all well and good, then a duty to your Manchester traders, and now you say you have a duty to the tribes themselves. Maud, are you sure it's not something more than duty that makes you want to go back to them? Maybe you're idealizing the tribes."

"I should hope not," she said quickly. Then she added after a pause, "Aside from everything—what they've given me, what I've given them—there is something else. You're right. I don't know what to call it but when I'm writing about the tribes, even taking down notes, I'm happy, truly happy. There's a sense of satisfaction. An ineffable happiness that I can't describe. It's as though I've left this sordid world behind and entered another realm, a realm of supreme pleasure, a realm of aesthetic wonder and beauty. I don't know, David, if I'm making sense."

I said nothing. What could I say? Of course she made sense. Too much sense, in fact. I felt as if I had run into a stone wall. When I picked up the conversation again she was talking about the Colonial Office. They wanted a full account of whom she'd spoken to, and what was said. What deals she'd made. "Imagine. Whitehall Street bloody well thinks I'm a spy."

I broke my silence. "Damn Whitehall, damn the Colonial Office, Maud. They just want to see what it takes to put you down. You've ruffled so many feathers. You've made enemies. It's the price of civilization." My fear that I was losing my grip on her caused me to speak more harshly than I intended.

The oaks swayed in the wind and the sparrows stayed hidden in the brown leaves. "And a mighty tall price it is," she said, stopping in her tracks and shaking her head, disturbed at my remark, as if I had joined her detractors. "Civilization, you call it, this England. I call it a cage, complete with iron bars. Really, David. Civilization is supposed to allow people to make contact with their souls. But our society is a separator."

We continued walking. "You've lived in London now. You see, you hear. Cardboard people everywhere, with painted smiles and painted frowns. And if you happen to be a woman, you're drenched in humility. Yesterday you asked me what I wanted to be free from. Remember? And I said, from being a woman. Last week I had to give a report to the Scottish Geographical Society in Edinburgh. Imagine now, all that I learned of tribal spiritualism, of tribal laws and customs, not easily acquired material, as you well know. The swamps, the mosquitoes, the hot, sleepless nights; it was all there, in that report, the sweat of three years. Yet when it came to be read, I had to hand it over to a man. A woman in this civilized land of ours is not permitted to address a scientific body. And you know the saddest part? I never so much as blinked when I handed it over."

Anger swelled within me. "You shouldn't have let them have it if you couldn't read it yourself."

"I surrendered, David, what more can I tell you. I surrendered. There are only so many icons I can break."

"And it's made you bitter," I said, "mostly with yourself."

We continued our walk but I don't remember where we went or what we saw. I had withdrawn into myself. My competition was not some bureaucrat in the Colonial Office, but with the tribes themselves, with what they had given her. She had said they transported her to another realm. She had called it a realm of wonder and beauty. And it had hit me like a stone wall because I knew I could not follow her there.

That evening was a memorable one for me, for many reasons; for one, it was the first time I had been in a limousine. The Art Society sent one to pick us up. I wore the best suit I had and Maud wore a one-piece woolen outfit and high heels that made her appear even slimmer than she was. And as a favor to me, she unwound her hair and let it flow past her shoulders. I thought she looked grand.

The limo brought us to Kensington Hall, which served as Mayfair's convention and cultural center. The place had been bequeathed to the Society by an important family. The grounds were spacious, well landscaped, with tennis courts and a croquet field.

As we entered the hall several of the Society's ladies, all in long gowns and with faces that resembled Afghan hounds, embraced Maud and whisked her away without taking the slightest notice of me. I checked my coat, and as the town's big shots, ju-jus, Maud called them, engaged her in deep conversation, I viewed the oil paintings of castles and gardens that hung on the walls. I could see what was going on. These people were Maud's neighbors, her own people. Perhaps it was a mistake to have come with her. Bringing me along would only make things more difficult for her.

Meanwhile, the hall was quickly filling up. The musicians seated near the main table in front of the huge bay window began tuning their instruments. I took a chair where I could find one, at a table in the back. Maud was seated at the main table in front of the bay window with the ju-jus.

Then she spotted me, excused herself, got up and crossed the floor and reached for my hand. "David," she said, "I don't know if you've noticed but right here, before our eyes, is the staunch wall of Mayfair's haute society. You've got to help me get through this night. Please join me, will you?"

"There's no room at your table," I said. "Besides, I have the feeling I'm persona non grata as far as Mayfair's haute society goes."

She pulled me from my chair. "As far as I'm concerned, Davey, you're persona grata. Come join me."

I could see by her eyes that she meant it. I took her extended hand and ignored the hundred faces that followed my footsteps as I walked to the main table.

"Bring us another chair, will you, Billy?" she said to a starchy young fellow standing there.

"Yes, ma'am," he answered, and he hurried off, promptly returning with a chair.

And so I was seated. Maud introduced me, and there were nods and mumbles all around. Then one of the ladies, a secretary of the committee, asked Maud if I was a nephew of hers, or perhaps a cousin.

"David Unger belongs to neither species. He's a very special friend."

The secretary lifted a brow. Maud responded to her puzzlement with an assured smile.

Drinks were brought out, and then our dinner was served—a typically overdone roast. During the meal people chatted and gossiped. Some heads turned my way, to get a better look at Maud's special friend, to gauge my age, I suppose. I was proud of Maud, of the way she took my hand whenever it pleased her, the way she stood up to them.

When dinner was over, the teapots were passed and tea was poured. Then the committee president struck the side of his glass with a fork to gain everyone's attention and introduced Maud. "The flower of Kent, returned to us at last." Polite applause followed.

Maud stood up. She had no slides, no maps, no graphs, no prepared speech. She wasn't to give a lecture, only a small, impromptu talk. And as she launched into her discussion, I could almost hear the plaintive sighs. This was a gathering of townspeople, of Maud's own neighbors. They wanted to hear about how happy she was to be home and how she appreciated England. They didn't at all want to hear about Africa. They'd already read as much as they wanted to know about Maud's time in that dreaded place in the papers.

But they received no succor from Maud that evening. In fact, the gist of her remarks condemned the Africa Crown Colony Office. British interests in Africa, she said, should be confined to the sphere of trade. Britain should not be playing political banjo games. "Africa is for the Africans," she said, "and is not a European playground." A genteel applause followed her talk.

Then came the questions. How did the heathen, polygamous marriages compare with marriage among civilized people? African marriages were altogether happier, Maud said. "The several wives the tribesmen have make for a lighter workload for each, which allows them free time for themselves. This is definitely something the females should look into," she said with an incredibly straight face. In terms of fidelity, it goes without saying, she declared, the tribesman with several wives has little need to tomcat—unlike his English counterpart.

Many faces went red there and quite a lot of muttering followed. Someone noted that the newspapers had hailed her as the New Woman. Could she comment? She could. She promptly derided the New Woman idea. She cooked her own food, mended her own clothes and regarded the coast traders her mentors.

The "new women" in the audience bristled; they wanted acquiescence on the part of their guest and when they realized they weren't going to get it, they fired their moral salvos at Maud. How could she travel on Africa's oil rivers in the company of those ruffian palm oil traders, former slave traders, some of them? With men who consorted with the native women? They had also heard that she cursed like a trooper and smoked tobacco and that she was against the liquor tax.

She was against all taxes that subjugated one people to the whims of another. The liquor tax, she said, was a racist gambit that fed the notion of white superiority over blacks—as if only the Europeans could drink beer and wine without dire consequences. As for the other charges, yes, she smoked on occasion. As for cursing—how else could she let off steam at the foggy notions that came out of Parliament and Whitehall Street?

Concerning her living with traders, true, they were a rough bunch and they drank a lot, but they would never insult a woman, which was more than she could say for Britain's learned societies who would not allow a woman, any woman, to read a scientific paper to them.

It was quite a night for Maud. I think everyone was relieved when the music began. Before very long the floor became crowded with couples. Maud nudged me with her elbow and we got up. I took her hand and led her to the dance floor. We swung out, hand in hand and holding each other's waists, whirling under the bright lights. I can still see her smiling face. I think she was even singing. I know she was very happy. On this occasion, she had not surrendered.

When we returned to Crossgate we built a fire and lay on the rug before the fireplace, and in the sparkling firelight I removed her clothes and she removed mine and we huddled under the afghan. I touched her breasts, her stomach. I touched her brow and her eyes lightly, as a stone carver might, to discern the secret hollows of her face. My fingers traced a tiny throbbing vein that ran down her neck and into her chest bone's cavity. Her smile, which had pleased me so much all evening, troubled me now in our love making—for I felt that her mind was still at Kensington Hall, reliving the pleasure of non surrender.

I have always felt that sex is the most impersonal of feelings, the one feeling that least belongs to us as individuals. I have always felt that we belong to sex rather than the other way around. We are its captors, carried along with the promise of a joy that is never enough, or is utterly enough but for only for a moment. We partake of sex, exploit it, harbor it, withhold it, sell it, buy it—yet it doesn't belong to us.

What I wanted to give her was not my impersonal sex, but that which truly belonged to me to give. Sex was too public, too transient. I wanted to give my heart. And I wanted the same of her. But sex—and the implications of her smile, perhaps—stood in the way. Sex blocked the exchange I longed for.

Sex separated us and left us each alone. In our silent embrace, it joined us in body but not in soul.

When we were done, her breathing evened and she moved her arm and I withdrew myself from her. She came to her elbow. The firelight's shadows played off her face. She asked me why I was sad.

"You're beyond me now," I mumbled. And then I could not stop myself. I told her I knew she would leave soon and that I would not see her again.

She answered with silence.

We stayed together the entire night, but it was not enough.

The following day we packed lunch, hitched a horse that we had borrowed from one of the neighbors to a two-wheel buggy and rode out toward Canterbury. Maud wore a herringbone tweed outfit and a feathered hat. I teased her about it, but in fact it gave me the chance to glimpse what she might have been like had she remained Maud King of Mayfair instead of becoming Maud King the explorer. And I could not help but ask myself if I would have loved her had I met her in England instead of Africa. Did I love Maud King, the woman, or did I love the role she played?

By the time we reached the high country, the sky had cleared and we stopped to have lunch on a hill. It was quite beautiful—the tall oaks, the gnarled yews, centuries old, swaying in the autumnal wind. We heard the Canterbury bells call out across the gentle countryside, and below, as if in response to that call, groups of pilgrims, some on horseback, some on foot, made their way toward the famous cathedral.

From where we were we could see the split in the River Stour where one part flowed around a wall and the other part, hidden, went through the town itself. On the banks of the river, where the sea trout came up from the channel and broke water from time to time, stood the neatly timbered homes of the weavers. Soft and solemn the bells tolled.

I took Maud's hand.

"I know what you're thinking," she said. "You'd rather we lived together here in Canterbury, or even in Mayfair." Her hair stirred in the wind. She had told me that morning that she had decided to return to Africa—not right away, but as soon as her obligations in London were taken care of. I knew there was no chance that she would change her mind, but I had made that my purpose anyway.

"Maud," I said, "you are all that's real in my life. Everything else is like my stage tricks, based on illusions. But apparently you don't feel the same way."

"David, I've thought about us making a life together. But last night was a sample of what our life in England would be."

"You never cared about them before."

"For myself, I don't. But if you're to be a doctor someday, you need the respect of people, not their derision."

"Respect be damned."

She regarded me closely. "My dearest David, you are the most important person in my life. You know that. But ours is a selfish love, the kind that wouldn't benefit either of us."

"A life apart from you is no life. And not your age or my age or all the damn people in London or Mayfair can change that. Your leaving will turn my heart to stone."

"Whatever stands in the way of your education is wrong."

"My feelings for you can never be wrong. My father was a doctor, but in his last days he worked as a common laborer, in a pit. What did his schooling get him? My mother left him. I left him. He died alone, a complete failure."

Before she could respond, I drew her to me and kissed her. And it was only after the bells were silent a while that I realized how completely I had lost myself in our embrace.

We made it back to Mayfair that evening, cold, tired and hungry. We cooked a warm meal on her great stove and drank wine.

"Yours is a self-imposed exile," I muttered.

"Please," she sighed.

I could see my resistance was only annoying now; Maud had had enough of it. I raised my glass. "May the Africa you are returning to be worthy of your devotion." She stared at me for a long time. Then she raised her glass too and we drank.

Chapter Seven

Maud's book on her African adventures came out shortly after our weekend together, and she was roundly touted by the press. The British Museum opened a wing of her exhibit, and for a while she was the most famous woman in England. She made a grand tour of the British Isles and even the Queen invited her for a chat. I dropped in at the museum now and then, since it was well within walking distance of my West End flat.

Meanwhile I was accepted to Cambridge's School of Medicine. Maud offered me money from her royalties, but I refused. I knew this time she was going to Africa not as a trader invoiced by Tobin and Blackstone, her English firm, or by the Black Forest outfit, her German purveyor, but rather solely under the auspices of the British Museum. And I knew the museum had awarded her barely enough to cover her passage to Africa, not nearly enough to subsist on, and so I refused her kindness. Besides, I told her, my nightclub work paid me well. I had no need for assistance. We let it go at that.

We saw each other on and off several more times, moments stolen from our busy lives—once at the theater, another time at a train station and finally during a commencement exercise at King's College. When the spring semester began, I gave up my West End flat and went to Cambridge. And Maud quietly sailed for the dark continent. I had planned to see her off, but somehow there was a schedule mix up, and when her boat left Liverpool I was not with her. I had gotten there too late. Her other friends and associates had already left, I was told, her Strand publicist, and the few relatives she had. If there's such a thing as a low point in one's life, mine was on that day.

The empty feeling continued. In the months that followed I struggled to attend classes. Perhaps what kept me going was the one letter I received from her. I got it about a month after she'd landed on the coast of Africa. The letter was postmarked from Libreville in Gabon. In it she wrote that she missed me very much and it was her most fervent hope, if I were not married by the time she got back, and if I'd still have her, that we might try to make a go of it. It was a lovely letter, but I could not be sure that it was not merely my consolation prize— offered to me to make up for the fact that she was gone.

Yet, how many times I read that letter, awakening from sleep in the dead of night full of the hope of her promise. She was always on my mind, and hardly a night went by that she didn't occupy my dreams.

I worried, I waited, but no further word of her came.

Out of sight, out of mind, they say, and as far as the newspapers went, they soon found other people to write about. Now and then her name cropped up, mostly in one of the scholarly magazines—not often, then hardly at all.

As for me, I continued to do an act or two at the London clubs on weekends; and I even ran into my old friend Wimpenny once, who had moved to London. We had a few beers and talked over old times. He informed me that my mentor Bapu had become quite popular in India. "The top dog spiritual leader," was how he put it.

"But is he top dog in religion or politics?" I asked.

"You think there's any real difference?"

He asked me if I still saw Maud King; I had told him all about her long ago, in the cave. I explained that I had lost out to the "wonder and beauty of Africa." Then Wimpenny came back to Gandhi. "He may have taken a poverty vow, but inside himself he's the richest man on earth. He's like Mozart living in squalor but all the while creating beautiful castles of music. These kinds of people, they can transcend their own humble lot in life. Who knows. Your Maud King may be one of that same breed.

"Like the lions," he continued. "This transcendence thing is like that, only on a higher plane. Putting down your badness, elevating what's good in you. Not just stepping down to a tree stump but reaching up too. It's spooky, this trying to become only the good in yourself. It's like becoming a bloody saint. But I think that's what your Gandhi is after. And from the sounds of it, maybe your Maud King is after the same thing. I don't know."

School took up most of my time. I wrote Maud letters, so many letters, but, as I had nowhere to send them, I put them away in a drawer. In my imagination we had the most wonderful conversations. I imagined us going to all sorts of places, meeting all kinds of people. The nurturing of this fantasy kept me from despair.

The silent months rolled into a year, then two years. Perhaps she had already returned, I thought, and was walking the London streets unnoticed and alone. I had all sorts of weird ideas. I just couldn't imagine her trekking into the African interior—in spite of the fact that she had done it before. No news was good news, I told myself.

And so it went.

In my third year of medical school I got a job on weekends at St. Elizabeth's Hospital in London. I did odd jobs, whatever was needed. If they asked me to wash out bedpans, that was my job that night. From time to time I inquired at the museum about Maud's whereabouts, in the hope that some news had turned up. But nothing did. They said that after she had reached the African coast, she had sent the museum lots of noteworthy specimens, then the specimens stopped coming and she hadn't been heard from since.

This kind of chilling news made me all the more anxious to track her down. I remembered she used to bank at Barclay's and so I contacted the Bloomsbury branch and asked where they sent Maud King's statements. They had not done business with her in some years, they said. Her account was closed. They had no idea where she was. I called on her cousin Rita Anthony, the children's writer. She also hadn't a clue as to Maud's whereabouts. All Rita knew was that she herself paid the taxes on the old house. None of Maud's other relatives knew anything either.

A great darkness came into my life, and I spent hours at the Cambridge library staring at maps of West Africa. Was she still out there somewhere? Why didn't she return home? What had happened to her? I walked the streets a ghost of my old self, searching the eyes of every tall, slender woman I passed.

Then it happened, the totally unexpected.

One night my work at the hospital was to put together batches of medical supplies for shipment overseas—a menial task, an order clerk's job in any department store. The hospital had a contract with an international agency—something like the Red Cross—and this agency was dedicated to providing medical care in the old British and French territories, India, Asia and of course, Africa.

As I was entering a thick batch of order requests into a ledger, something caught my eye. It was a small yellow order form from a field clinic in the French Congo, from a place called Makokou. At the bottom of the order list was Maud King's signature.

My department supervisor was a short Scotsman, MacHenry was his name. He had a swirl of red hair plastered over the back of his head like a yarmulke and he wore slippers. I approached him with the rush order.

He knew of the order, he said. The hospital had been sending medical supplies to the Makokou clinic for over two years. "Just north of the zero line." A severe lupus epidemic had ravaged the Makokou area and Maud King was out there trying to keep the disease from spreading. "You may have heard of her," he said.

"She's a friend of mine," I replied.

Under lowered red lashes, the Scotsman said, "Is she now? Well, it's vaccines, drugs, bandages, medical instruments, that sort of thing's what she wants."

MacHenry looked me in the eye. "She was once quite the woman. Always kicking up her heels with the Crown, raising hell in Parliament. You'd think she'd have had her fill of Africa."

He shuffled to a cabinet and pulled her file. Her early memos were routine. But the last few were different. Her needs were for quinine and pain killers. I noticed her handwriting had become more angular, as if her hand was shaky when she wrote.

"How long will it take for the King shipment to get to Makokou?" I asked. I was already formulating a plan.

"Well, it's all paid for," said the Scotsman, "so it travels first class. Upwards of three months, I'd say. Could even be a hundred days."

"I'll get it there in two months, under two months," I said. "Advance me the postage money to put towards my passage and I'll guarantee delivery in half your time. How's that?"

The Scotsman stepped back astonished. "You're not serious? Such a thing is unheard of, going all the way to Africa. And what about your classes, or doesn't that matter? You'd never get back in time for your finals, you know. Why in the world would you want to do that?"

"Humanitarian motives," I said quickly. "Many lives can be saved if the delivery time is shorter. Please."

"Humanitarian, you say? Well, well, well. A friend of Maud King, you call yourself. A mite more than that, I'd say. This request you're making is highly irregular, you know that, don't you?"

"Doctor MacHenry, Maud King is no ordinary woman. I can be on the next boat out. Otherwise this order will take three weeks just to get out of the mailroom."

"Well, you're right about that much. I don't know. Highly irregular."

"There's little time to lose."

MacHenry shook his head and walked out into the hall. He came back in a while with a tray of food, which he placed on his desk. Then laying his hand on my shoulder, he said, "You know your own mind, David Unger, and I'm not going to pry. Just suffice it to say, I trust you. I'll recommend your request if you've not changed your mind by then. As for your classes…"

"The classes can wait," I said. "You have my undying gratitude, sir. And you can be certain I won't change my mind." I gave him a hearty handshake.

The old doctor touched his brow in wonder—or maybe dismay. "In that case, laddy," he said, "we'd better start with your malaria shots, hadn't we?"

Once I gave my medical school notice that I was taking a sabbatical, I returned to London, drained my bank account, went to a Bond Street travel agent and booked passage on a cargo vessel bound for West Africa out of Liverpool (the same Royal African line that Maud had taken). I then arranged for the entire Makokou-bound hospital shipment, a two-hundred-pound crate, to be sent by rail to the Liverpool dock.

That done, I canceled my nightclub engagements and in surrendering the keys to my flat, I told my landlady I was leaving England for an indefinite period. She said she'd hold my mail until I got back. Whenever that was. I packed some clothes and my carbine, grabbed an express train north and finally from the stern of the departing ship, the Duke of Marlborough, I waved England goodbye.

I had swiftly and quite efficiently arranged for my departure, but once on board the ship, time dragged. Every hour on the water was one hour less I would be with Maud, every day, one day less. It anguished me to think of how much time we had spent apart, I at Cambridge, and she operating a clinic in the middle of Africa. I might have known.

The ship entered tropical waters. The days grew warmer and the midday sun became a brilliant 24-carat chunk of gold. The nights were a mass of stars with a moon that stalked the ship like a pale ghost. I had the feeling I was on a rescue mission.

At each port of call, the ship's carpenter exploded gun powder so the harbor people would know we had arrived, and looking beachward, those of us on deck would see the shore buildings, dim, sun-bleached wooden structures with tin roofs that seemed ready to fade into the solid jungles behind them or melt into the surf-bound beaches. Visual illusions, they appeared, without substance or solidity. The only thing that seemed real was the fact that I was on my way to see Maud.

Finally the ship anchored at Douala to exchange cargoes. I roamed the streets, crowded with the Arab tribes of the Sudan. As fate would have it, I ended up at the same French shop where years before I had bought Maud's straw hat. This time I selected a suit, a smart linen outfit with brass buttons, and had it boxed. Imagining her opening it gave me a moment of happiness in an otherwise tedious journey.

The ship continued toward the equator, "the hot breath of death," as it was called. We were passed by a noisy British troop ship. The Boer War had started in South Africa, and the soldiers on the ship were having a terrific time with rifle practice. Their only problem was there were no targets in the middle of the ocean, so they simply shot at the waves.

After two weeks on the water, we docked at Libreville, with its palm trees and paved roads. There I inquired at a French colonial office about hiring some carriers to help me into the interior.

The director, grateful that I had let him finish his siesta, waived the fifteen sous license on my carbine and procured for me four Bapouonians at twenty-five francs apiece. Brothers they were. They had worked in a French iron mine. Atooko, the oldest, with flaring nostrils and a gold front tooth, was the spokesman. His brothers, I soon learned, were nearly deaf, having lost their hearing in a mine blast.

According to my crude map, Makokou was two hundred and fifty miles due east in the upper reaches of the Ogooue

River, on a tributary known as the Djoud. I had never been on this river before, but I had a good compass, a sturdy axe, sharp knives and my well-oiled, license-free carbine. And of course I had determination. Atooko and I broke the medical supply crate into four neat parcels, which meant each man would carry fifty pounds on his back.

For two days we motored across a flat, salty terrain, then we climbed aboard an elephant and made ourselves comfortable in a bamboo chariot with a straw canopy that was strapped to the beast's back and rode across the steamy, malarial swamps of the coastal lowlands.

At Kango we took a steamer up the Ogooue to a muddy, feverish island called Ndjole. The island was mostly under water during the wet season and generally considered the last vestige of civilization before the higher elevations began. At Ndjole a sick Catholic missionary gave me his rather large canoe. The poor fellow, he was headed back to Brussels more dead than alive and he issued a sardonic smile when I offered him money. He counted what I gave him and handed it back, as if suggesting that where he was going he had no need of money.

We secured the four parcels of supplies firmly in the canoe. Then I sat behind the carriers and we started up the Ogooue, an eastward course, into the blistering sun of the open country, then into the jungle.

At times the river narrowed for miles and the trees on the left and right banks arched high over the middle of the river, their interlocking branches shutting out the sun so entirely that we traveled for hours in a green twilight. Given a little imagination, you could imagine that you were traveling at the bottom of the sea.

When the river widened again, the sun at the water's edge shone with renewed power. Twisting vines and thorny creepers flourished, binding trees and shrubbery together with such skill that the jungle seemed a forbidden, matted, solid thing. My Bapouonians pulled on their oars, their muscular backs gleaming with sweat. How I wished I still possessed my old launch, Land's End. I'd have stopped off at the academy and taken it with me, but knowing the authorities there had deemed it unseaworthy even when I had it, I figured they had surely let the engine rust out.

Toward evening the "smokes" came up, woolly mists that made it impossible to see the hand in front of your face, let alone the flitting cannibal tribesmen known as the Fangs. Atooko said the Fangs were hostile to Bapouonians and often disguised themselves as leopards when they ripped out their victim's entrails. That being the case, my weary companions hunkered down in the canoe and tried as best they could to ignore the sounds of the night.

There are many night sounds on a jungle river. Besides the more than occasional fish jumping out of the water, there is the whir of rushing crabs and, inland, the noise of romping elephants breaking branches or rubbing against groaning trees; now and then there is the sudden sigh of a hippo. Even the crocs make noise, if only an occasional cough. They move silently enough, though. What gives them away is their musty odor. And judging from the odor that night, there were plenty of them around.

At dawn our canoe mounted the savage rapids in the high country and our paddles flew at top speed to avoid the underwater razor sharp rocks that could slice right into the bow. Beyond the rough water the river widened and we made good time, ten, fifteen miles a day. Sometimes we saw Pygmies up on the ridges, hostile ones who shot small arrows in our direction for no apparent reason. Strange, I had always traveled safely among them before. Perhaps they were being territorial and resentful of my Bapouonian companions. A few shots from my Martini-Henry, however, kept them at too great a distance to do any damage.

At Booue our luck ran out. The village consisted of missionary quarters, two or three trading buildings, a few black traders' huts along the river, and a public house with lodgings. For most travelers it was only a one-day stopover. In the lodging house we met a French-speaking Arab ivory trader. Hamed something or other was his name, and he was a fleshy fellow in a sweat-ringed turban who was very impressed that Atooka could count.

Hamed had an infuriating habit. He was always fidgeting. Even when standing perfectly still, something in him was not at rest. He had a concubine, a veiled, sloe-eyed negress called Fala. He rented her in exchange for favors—a ride down the river, a few rounds of ammunition, fresh water, things of that sort. I took an instant dislike to him.

Throughout the day hardly an hour went by that Hamed

wasn't invoking Allah. "Inshallah" this, "Inshallah" that. God willing this, God willing that. According to the missionaries, Hamed was a Sonniki, a liberal Mohammedan who, despite his advanced views, played it safe and never failed to recite the Dhiker toward Mecca before nightfall, just in case his Allah was of the conservative persuasion. He also carried a fancy sidearm and drank a lot.

That evening in the public house our liberal Sonniki made me a proposition. He wished to swap his Fala for "the nigger Atooka." He assured me in the most spittle-besotted French I had ever heard that behind her veil Fala was a woman of many charms and quite learned in the ways to please a man. She stood behind him, a small, lithe creature as silent as Atooka's brothers. She tried to say something once and he admonished her sharply, "Malesh, malesh," he said. Never mind, never mind.

"No deal," I told him.

"Then you rent Atooko to me, and I rent you Fala, only for tomorrow. "No deal," I said again. He studied me with oily eyes. I was wise to him. His plan was to sell Atooko to slavers the first chance he got. Apparently he didn't care what happened to Fala. I cautioned Atooko to stay away from him.

It rained that night; there was lightning and thunder and high winds like those a tornado makes when it uproots trees. And while the Bapouonians slept in the next room from mine, a sound of sandals stopped at my door, and as the winds hurled a river of water against the tin roof of the public house, a light-footed creature, with a swinging lantern in her hand

and a veil across her face, soundlessly entered my room, turned the light of her lantern down low and removed her veil and proceeded to disrobe.

"What are you doing?" I asked.

She whispered something and tiptoed to my bed. She sought a safe place to put the lantern. When her hand touched my shoulder, I grabbed her lantern and pushed her aside. Then I rushed out into the hall, kicked open the Arab's door, and finding his room abandoned, I ran out into the howling storm.

Lightning flashed and thunder roared. The winds wailed with the agonized voices of fiends who have climbed over the brim of hell. Too late. On the black velvet shore, under a storm-bent tree, were the dumped contents of my canoe. The canoe itself was only a bucking, dim light on the swollen river. The Arab inside it was undoubtedly paddling fiercely and already beyond reach.

That night no one got much sleep. In the lodging house I tried to cut a deal for another canoe. There were several canoes in the village that belonged to the traders and the missionaries, but they were all used on a daily basis. They weren't for sale, which was the very reason the pious Hamed had stolen mine.

By morning the rain had stopped. Fala, no longer wearing her veil, came to me while Atooko and I were discussing what to do next.

"I belong to you now," she said in broken French, rubbing her eyes.

"No Fala," I replied, "you're free."

"I am not free."

I could see her point. When Hamed took ownership of my canoe, he relinquished ownership of Fala. That meant as long as Hamed had my canoe, she belonged to me. In her eyes at least. "No, Fala," I said, "your slave days are over. You're free." I shook my head. My canoe had paid for her freedom.

"You no like me?" she persisted

"Don't get me wrong, Fala. I like you fine. But you don't belong to me or to Hamed. You belong to yourself. You're a free woman."

"You not be fair," said Atooko, his gold tooth reflecting brightly the morning sun. "Hamed steal your canoe, you take his woman." Where Atooko came from, a man paid heavily to buy a wife. With Hamed giving me a wife for the taking, he thought me stupid for not taking her, only he didn't want to call me stupid, so he said I wasn't being fair.

"No, Atooko," I said.

Atooko frowned. "You see," he said. "You be sorry."

I ignored him and unrolled a map. We had reached the Djoud tributary where the waters were shallow. The Bapouonians gathered around me murmuring incoherently. They felt terrible about the canoe. I told Atooko we needed to concentrate; what was done couldn't be undone and we had best start working on continuing our journey.

That same morning we built a raft of axed logs held tight with bush ropes. By midday, after bidding a forlorn Fala good luck and farewell, we began poling our way upriver.

My companions were sullen. No matter what I said they couldn't reconcile to the fact we now had to travel on a slippery raft instead of a safe, roomy canoe. Yet, they were grateful that I had not compromised their freedom, which would have been the case had I exchanged Atooko, Hamed's original choice, for Fala. They leaned on their poles with stiffened arms, drawing in the river bottom, intermittently shaking their fists at the sky whenever they thought of the Arab thief. And Atooko invoked the names of so many spirits that if he had awakened only a fraction of them, the pious Hamed would have been haunted the rest of his life.

We were traveling on the equator now, and the heat was the devil's own. When it rained the humidity increased and sharpened the attacks of the savage mosquitoes and the pestering mangrove flies. I reminded myself that the only thing that mattered was seeing Maud again.

We traveled the better part of a month like this. At first we ate from tins, then later we trapped snakes, caught fish and even speared some fowl. At times we left the river, especially when we heard the tom-toms of the Fangs or spotted their bark huts. Other times we found ourselves tide trapped, our brown waterway having turned into a mucky swamp, and rather than pull across miles of thick malarial mud and leeches, we ditched our raft and hauled the supplies on our shoulders. Through the tall sword grass, dense stuff, ten, fifteen feet high, we went, then waded into the finer hippo grass until we reached the bank itself. There we fought thickets of screw pines, scratchy trees with sword-shaped leaves as sharp as a knife. They grew in clusters five feet, six feet long, these pines, with a network of embroidered aerial roots so embroidered that once they reached down into the water, no axe could cut through them.

On higher ground we made more headway. We slashed down rubbery vines and monstrous succulents and avoided the flattened undergrowth, which usually signaled the recent passing of a boa constrictor.

How I cursed Hamed when the river ran deep again and we had to build another raft.

The mangrove flies stung with bb-shot intensity, but Atooko and his brothers didn't seem to mind. They became accustomed to the raft as it slid over sharp rocks, and soon Atooko was singing and his brothers were dancing and amusing themselves with frightening stories. Their voices were loud when they spoke among themselves.

Atooko did a pantomime of the evil spirit Sasabonsum. No sacrifice could appease him. He lived where the silk cotton tree grew and where the earth was red with human blood. Sasabonsum! Witches and apparitions could not buy him off. Sasabonsum! He scorned charms. His wrath was terrible. His eyes saw everyone. Sasabonsum! His power was greater than the almighty Anzambe, the indifferent one. The Bapouonians leaned on their poles and laughed loudly, ever drawing on the river bottom.

At some point it seemed that we had eaten every kind of food the river could possibly provide. Our skin was covered with rashes, and our bowels cut raw with dysentery. We had been bitten by snakes and sucked on by leeches. We were exhausted. Atooko had almost lost an eye one morning when he reached for an egg in a hornbill's nest. And now, as we poled our way up the river, we suddenly heard the hacking of axes and the wheezing of saws. A gang of natives in loincloths was clearing a hillside for the planting of coffee trees. Atooko called out to them. Did the lumbermen know of a clinic in the area?

Surely, surely. Three days up the river, the great medicine lady's place, on the right fork. We guided the raft toward the bank. The tree cutters came down to meet us. They warned us the place had fallen under the power of Mbuiri, who governs many evil spirits. We were sure to regret it if we proceeded any farther. The tree cutters invited Atooko and his brothers to join them in clearing the land while the hiring boss was still around. The pay was good. Later they could work on the coffee plantation.

I told Atooko that the medicine inside our crates was more powerful than any of the evil spirits. He believed that strongly, he said, but it wasn't the spirits he feared. He and his brothers had an opportunity for jobs. They had to consider the future.

There was nothing I could say. My carriers accepted the tree cutters' offer. I couldn't blame them. The plantation was long-term, a clean job, better than the mines. So I paid them, and they each took my right hand and with great energy said the word "Ibata" three times, each time spitting into my palm for good luck.

What compelled Atooko and his brothers to join me in the first place, and to stick with me when the going got rough? No one would have faced the dangers of the Djoud for money alone. I had reason to go to Makokou. But my young travelers had no such reason. Yet they showed more alacrity in discharging their duties than the staunchest of allies. Why?

As I prepared to travel forward on my own, I recalled that Maud had once told me that certain proud tribesmen, after the white man destroyed their belief in the fetish and their place in nature, would strive against this displacement by taking on only the most difficult work, as if only such tasks were capable of reshaping their broken inner lives and enabling them to regain their lost stature. Europeans, she'd argued, were concerned with the material world of nature, while all that mattered to the African was the internal, spiritual self.

Chapter Eight

That afternoon, as I continued up the river, the tom-toms started, an alternately short and long hypnotic beat that throbbed like an aching tooth. I wished for rain, for thunder or hail, for anything that would break the hot, humid air that surrounded my raft. The drums continued. From my association with Maud I was able to decipher their message; they told of the spread of death, of the great anger of the forest spirits, in fact, of the great evil that Atooko had imitated in his pantomime.

I drew the raft slowly up the shoal waters through masses of tropical grass. Drearily I poked at what seemed like a floating log until a crocodile suddenly snapped at my pole. A dry suffocating heat poured down from the sky. At midday I sought the shady waters along the bank. The tom-toms continued. When night came, my raft bobbed in the misty water, anchored by a stone. I lay against the crates, my carbine nearby. The tom-toms told their story over and over again. I tried to sleep, but a fever chilled my bones and kept me awake.

At dawn, with stiff, stretched arms, I poled through infusorial enclaves hazy with shapeless hulks of trees enshrouded in eerily floating mists and the luminous vapors that encircled the upper branches. Reptilian eyes, I was sure, followed my moves. Looking at my reflection on the water I hardly recognized the bearded, glaring, shaggy-haired, instinctual creature I had become. The Fangs, I could tell, were still about. The fleeting movements in the bush, the sudden, frightened flight of pelicans out of the hippo grass, were all signs of their presence. I sank my pole in deeper and drew on the river bottom. The sun's heat was dry, suffocating.

By midday it was as if a flame had set the sky itself on fire. In the afternoon the entire river was enveloped in a steamy vapor. I had drained my canteen and thus drank from the river freely. The drums started again, louder, and they brought a new message now; they told of my approach. The jungle hummed in harmony with their incessant beat.

In the late afternoon my fever flared as the sun's spikes of fire pierced my forehead and I sought whatever shade the bank might offer. I paused at pools of stagnant waters and noted the gloom of the inner forest thick with shadows and murky shafts of light. In these dark enclaves the trees seemed shapeless, shimmering hulks enshrouded in poisonous vaporous fingers that reached twenty, thirty feet into the first line of branches. Some trees were freshly scratched, a sign of leopards. Atooko had said the Fangs disguised themselves as leopards and ripped out their victim's entrails. I wondered if there were real leopards about, or were the Fangs stalking me?

On the main river again my raft passed the same solid wall of trees, unvarying in color, in form, in height. Islands of grass and a lettuce-like substance surrounded the craft. I was glad

I was not in my old launch now, for no screws could turn in that mass, and I had to lean hard on the pole to push through. When night came I again tossed my stone anchor overboard and my raft bobbed on the invisible water.

On the third night, as I lay curled against the heap of supplies, my carbine in the crook of my arm, my head full of broken bits of dreams and the sounds that frogs and insects make, I awoke with a start. The sky beyond the black tree tops was teeming with trembling stars. The moon glowed coldly on the milky still river. Back in the jungle a leopard coughed. I noticed a ripple in the water expanding from my raft. Above me came the thin cry of bats. I noticed too the front of the raft tilting downward. Crocodiles sometimes placed their long jaws on the raft's edge. Usually I poked them in the snout and they'd either snap at the pole or ease off.

This time though the raft dipped even lower in the water as if held under pressure, and I struck a lucifer match. And then as I reached for my pole, at the same time waving off a flight of bats (from the sound of their soft-flapping flight and their cries, there had to be hundreds of them), I saw there, but six feet away, under a flickering glare, a savage face with red eyes, scars across his brow and down the bridge of his nose and a gleaming knife stuck between pointy teeth. He was rising out of the water. A Fang. He was trying to pull himself onto my raft!

I shouted. My Martini-Henry flashed, recoiled against my shoulder and threw smoke into my eyes. The raft heaved and splashed. I stayed frozen in the echo of the rifle's roar. Had that savage climbed on board again, I'm sure I couldn't have moved a muscle. I have no idea how much time elapsed before I realized the Fang was gone. A minute, five minutes, ten minutes? He made no sound, but was gone, like a dream upon awakening. I heard my own heart beating loudly. Had the devil escaped under the raft, which was still quaking and full of motion? Was he wounded? Dead? The entire jungle, every frog, every insect, every living thing waited in stony silence for my next move. I probed the waters, but found nothing.

Then, as if on signal, the jungle noises started again, louder than before. It was as if my bullet had struck a box full of animal sounds and every noise in the jungle spilled out all at once—the whirs, the whining cries, the screams, the mournful wails.

It was no dream. The cannibal had wanted my rifle. My skin was not worth the risk. Or was it? Shaken, weary, I needed sleep. But I fought it off. As the woolly mists blanketed the raft, I lay suspended in a guarded twilight of stillness, my finger on the cocked carbine's trigger, watchful—and watched, I'm sure.

The arrival of dawn came slowly, just a few beams filtering through the trees that reached over the river. Then the screech of parrots and the hysterics of monkeys brought me to my feet and the darkness retreated from under the forest's dark canopy, and the jungle became a pale green effusion of light. Another day had come.

The smokes were particularly heavy that morning, lingering, slow to move on, but something was different; something had changed. Beyond the parrots and the hysterics of the monkeys there was silence. The drums that had told of my coming had stopped. I had spent many days on the ocean and many more traveling from the African coast into the interior. I had been bitten by crawling things and was suffering from dysentery and malaria. There were four types of malaria; that much I knew, and MacHenry's shots had prevented the two more common ones. My chills and fever every three days came from one of the less common types, that much I also knew. But I had reached my destination.

Poling my raft landward, I thought I heard a tree limb fall into the river. Then several crocodiles left the bank on the opposite shore and swam swiftly toward the center of the river. Around a bend came a canoe. In it were five skeletons, tribesmen who were surely shadows of their former selves, struggling to steady their rocking canoe. Nearby a body floated, face down, rotating in a lazy circle. It had been tossed from the canoe. I turned away as the first crocodile submerged the body with a loud snap. Even in my somnambulist state I couldn't bring myself to witness a man being eaten. When the other crocodiles reached the scene, there were furious grunts and slapping tails. The canoe men passed me with hardly a glance. They were so weak they barely kept their oars in the water. Really, the current carried them along.

Hardly able to stand on my feet, my eyes salty with sweat, I flung a bush rope around a tree and pulled the raft to the bank. In the water I struggled to keep my balance. Should I wait for a few of the villagers to come to fetch the medical supplies, or start inland and find Maud?

I grabbed my carbine and climbed out of the water, Maud's suit box tucked under my arm. I slowly plied my way through the gauze-like mists. Unseen roots tripped me and I reached for trees that weren't there. My feet, it seemed, had forgotten how to walk and my eyes were blind with a burning sweat. Finally, I stumbled and fell.

The next thing I knew I was on my knees. Someone had poured water on my head. I felt I had been unconscious for a month. "Hey mon, you find too much bad place to sleep."

A sooty-faced fellow with bright eyes and yellow teeth glared down at me. He wore a Panama hat. "Mboloani," I uttered. Greetings, or May you have a long life.

Three other blacks in sleeveless shirts and shorts stood behind the one in the Panama hat. "Ai Mbolo. Ai Mbolo," they said. I was still pretty groggy but clear enough to see I was in a cemetery, where the dead had been buried standing up, with their heads sticking up above ground. Most tribes buried their dead under mounds of sticks and leaves. I realized it was a human skull that had caused me to stumble.

Yes, I had reached the Ncomi village. At the mention of Maud King, "the medicine lady," Mister Panama Hat became animated. "Ya, ya," he exclaimed. "Ma be much sick. I be Rumbochembo. Most hoppy to be Ma's number one useful mon. Who you be?"

I told him I was a friend of Ma's, a friend of the medicine lady's. I told him this several times. Each time he shook his head. After several more rounds of introducing ourselves, with each making sure who the other was, I said, "Rumbochembo, can you take me to Ma? I bring medicine."

I pointed to the raft, and as Rumbochembo's men went to unload the supplies, their boss led me down a forest path. And with gestures, sighs and his own special brand of English (he had been to a mission school), he told me what had transpired at Makokou since Ma had become "much sick."

The air was heavy with the odor of ashes and I heard a distant drone, a dolorous hum. Dolorous: I call it that for it bespoke of a massively shared pain. Rumbochembo's story was gruesome. King Makokou was the ruler of the Ncomi people. Three years ago, he had let Ma set up a clinic in the village. The clinic did "much good stuff" and the local witch doctor, a gent called Quamxandi, went into exile. But now that this great sickness had devastated the region, Quamxandi was in business again in all his glory. He promised to return the land to the laws of the fathers, and King Makokou was helpless to stop him.

Rumbochembo hastened toward the village. "We no be for too long." He nodded at several small boxes on the footpath, asylums for souls that had been lured from their owners' during sleep. He then pointed to a tall cross among the trees' foliage. On one arm of the cross hung two stinking pieces of human entrails, horseflies buzzing around them. I think they were lungs and livers. The other arm held a row of dark fist-sized objects, shrunken faces, yes, wrinkled human faces reduced in size.

"Quamxandi's work?"

Rumbochembo said the witch doctor had made several slaves drink a purgative and in their vomit he found small lizards. Lizards meant evil spirits, so the slaves were sacrificed, a part of the new order since Ma became sick.

He said just two weeks ago Quamxandi had executed two women accused of adultery. The proof of their adulterous behavior, he said, was that their hands blistered after they were whipped through boiling palm oil.

There is no avoiding it, I thought, this sorcery, this evil spirit nonsense. It was like the humid smokes, the torrid heat, the demonic thunderstorms. It was everywhere. Maud had been wrong coming here to set up a clinic and getting caught in an epidemic. Why? Why had she done it? She had once said that she wanted to discover the African personality. At Mayfair she mentioned a sense of wonder and beauty. Well, what wonder and beauty was here in these hanging organs? In these shrunken heads? Weren't they too a part of the African personality, its fascination with superstition and witchcraft?

I followed Rumbochembo through a corridor of tall, thin trees bedecked with a hanging profusion of bush ropes, flowers and fronds, the odor of ashes growing stronger. Her clinic, I thought, was an aberration—a momentary lapse of sanity, like an opening in the rain forest that lasts but a short while until the trees grow back with a vengeance and the age-old darkness descends again.

It continued, that soft melancholy hum, behind the barking of dogs, it continued and no cry or screech could beat back or silence it, for it seemed the very origin, the inspiration, of life itself.

The village entrance was a gate in a fence of tightly grown saplings. The fetish charms and flowers hanging from its top, according to my guide, were to make bad spirits turn back.

Once through the gate we entered a smoky clearing in a wide circle of bamboo huts. The powdery mists, the drone of a shared pain, the spicy odor of ashes and burning flesh, it was all here now in force, and I felt I was entering a netherworld. The heavy, dank air was hard to breathe; it seemed more to belong to the river than the sky or the trees. I took labored steps, as one walking uphill, then I stopped. Smack in the middle of the clearing was a procession, a chanting chain of villagers with knotted rags pulled over scrawny buttocks and bony chests. Men, women and children holding bowls of plantains and other fruits emitted soft sobs; some moved slowly alongside tethered goats. Smoke and fires lit under kettles set on tripods were everywhere. By the sides of huts were piles of smoldering crocodile carcasses. Vultures nested in trees.

I had never seen the likes of this gang of natives before, a mass of humanity with lowered, opaque, feverish eyes and shivering faces, their arthritically twisted bodies covered with lupus lesions, large brownish nodules festering with pus, their skin so loose I wondered how it didn't slip off their bones. Some had ulcerated eye sockets that oozed yellow pus, with maggots crawling from one eye to the other. One poor fellow dragged a useless foot. A piece of bamboo had been inserted in place of a leg bone. Naturally the leg had withered around the bamboo and the wasted foot just hung from a tendon string.

And where was this pitiful human mass crawling to? To the sacrificial hut, to a low, mud structure topped with dry grass that stood at the end of the village. This hut, darkly silhouetted against a dusky, purple sky, was the place where some crazy bush spirit demanded the slaughter of the villagers' livestock.

I approached the human chain, Rumbochembo at my side, my carbine in hand and Maud's suit still tucked under my arm. Tribesmen with lowered heads and trembling lips made room for us. Not a sound body anywhere. From the limbs of the tall trees vultures took flight. It was a sight that the eyes of God had turned from.

Suddenly from one of the huts came a chant: "Shango! Shango! Shango!" And a chorus of mourners appeared, women with shaved heads and chalky white bodies. They wore amber bracelets and strings of leopard teeth around their necks.

"Shango! Shango!" Their voices escalated to a tearful wail. At the sharp beat of a drum the mourners fell to the ground in totally abject abasement and gazed at Shango's hut. Hyenas howled in the distance. In the trees the vultures beat their wings.

"Shango dying," whispered Rumbochembo. "Him family call him soul back to him body. You sabe? If him soul leave him body, him family must pay witch doctor to find him soul.

Shango, he be King Makokou brother."

I didn't really want to understand, but I did. The mourners' job was to keep the soul from leaving Shango's body, for an unattached soul was a dreadful thing. Ridiculous, of course, but given my surroundings and the situation, I thought it best to play along. At St. Elizabeth's Hospital in London so-called civilized people often made even more of a fuss over a man dying.

I looked for a hut different than the others; I looked for Maud's clinic. My mind was not normal—from lack of sleep. I was easily distracted, in need of rest. As for the natives in that solemn human chain, they watched Shango's hut—as did the mourners abjectly spread out on the ground. The drum banged louder once, twice, then abruptly stopped.

Then, from Shango's hut emerged the shining light, the redeemer of the Ncomi, the glorious Quamxandi. The witch doctor stepped forth, tall and bronzed, with precise steps, his every move seemingly a part of some ritual. For a moment, he stood perfectly still at the entrance of the hut under a horned buffalo head dyed with frightening colors, his arms and legs covered with charms and animal skins. His black eyes glanced about furtively. I swear he knew of my presence before he saw me. Then he pivoted ever so slightly, tilted his head a bit, the better to focus, I suppose, and locked his black eyes on me. He stared at me for a full minute. There was no mistaking his enmity toward me.

I felt the same way, an immediate dislike of someone you don't even know, or want to know. It's more than a dislike, really, it borders on revulsion. You feel yourself in the presence of a natural enemy. I was his enemy and he was mine. There was no mistaking the glowering, downward curl of his mouth, the intensity of his stare. It was quite frightening, that stare of his. But I had not spent two months crossing land and sea to be put off by a third-rate sorcerer. I stared back. There was a kind of cunning in his stare. Yes, a cunning, as though he coveted something. I thought it had to be my carbine.

Then, abruptly, he threw his knees up high and came down in a sort of jump, and he repeated this movement faster and faster, with great deliberation. As he danced, he jabbed his fists skyward, shaking a bell and moving from hut to hut.

Damn fool, I thought. I had spotted what had to be Maud's clinic by then, a hut somewhat broader than the others. From a long stick on its roof hung a limp white flag with a blue star. Right next to the flag sat a nesting chicken. I was about to step back into Maud's life. I felt as though my life prior to that moment counted for nothing.

Rumbochembo touched me with his elbow, as might an all-knowing father who had a terrible secret to tell. "Him want you eyes."

Had I heard what I thought I heard? It made no sense to me, so I ignored the remark. My mind was elsewhere.

My companion, of course, knew nothing of my state at that moment, of my apprehension of meeting Maud again after four long years, and thus he thought it only proper to tell me what was going on. When the witch doctor's bell stopped tinkling before one of the huts, Rumbochembo leaned toward me and said that that was the hut in which the guilty family lived. "Guilty of what?" I asked. For the dying man's sickness, of course.

Had I been less irritable I might have taken the situation more seriously. But as it was, I was standing in a merciless tropical heat, amidst the stench of rotting human livers and crocodile innards and God only knows what else, in the shadow of buzzards glaring down from high trees, surrounded by a chain of sick moaning bodies, a flock of mourners at my feet, barking dogs and howling hyenas. What could I care about a tinkling bell? It seemed a stupid trifle. Later I would realize the serious consequences of Quamxandi's antics. But at that moment I thought the whole business no more than a sham. And anyway, I'd seen enough.

I was about to enter Maud's clinic when another flock of chalky mourners from the hut's interior rushed past me, casting hard glances at me as if I were a devil. Rumbochembo quickly explained it is forbidden for the mourners to be in the same house with a stranger. What did I care? Once inside the hut, in the shadowed coolness of that place, the outside world faded; I was in another realm. I was in Maud's presence. In the subdued light were several vacant cots, a batch of chairs, two tables and a quite empty medicine cabinet.

I felt Maud's nearness; it had a calming effect on me and broke the tension I had felt in my bones since I had started this journey. Then I saw her and I caught my breath. Maud was by the front window, asleep, her body wrapped in a white smock under a large mosquito net. She seemed at peace, her

repose serene, as if she were taking an afternoon nap. I silently moved closer.

I bent closer. She stirred, as if sensing my presence. I knelt
at her side. She looked beautiful to me, and youthful, despite
the dehydration, the pallor of her sunken face. A high fever
can sometimes have that effect. I looked for symptoms of her
illness. She didn't have lupus, or the sleeping sickness, that
much I could tell; maybe she had malaria. God knows she had
survived lots of that in her day. I kissed her warm folded
hands.

Then I saw them.

There comes a time when we refuse to believe our eyes,
and for me this was one of those times. I saw the rose spots
on her chest, and my mind went blank. A voice inside me said
I had not seen what I had seen and I turned away. Maud King
was in the advanced stage of enteric fever—typhoid.

How I hated Africa at that moment. Africa had taken Maud
from me and crushed her with this dreaded disease. My heart
turned to stone, the way it had when my father had said to me,
"Your mother is gone." Kneeling at Maud's bedside with the
same bitter tears that I'd shed for my mother, I vowed never
to leave Maud again.

I was full of recriminations. If only I had not let the Arab
at Booue steal my canoe. If only I had started sooner. Two
weeks would have made a significant difference.

Outside, among the huts, the shouting reached a shrill
pitch.

Maud's pulse was weak, her breathing labored. Her eyelids

flickered. After a few minutes she muttered aloud. I took her hand in mine. She opened her eyes. I touched her hot, damp brow.

"It's me, David," I said.

"David," she whispered through barely parted lips. She tried to rise, but failed. Tears came to her eyes.

"Don't try to talk," I said. "I've come to make you well again."

Her breathing momentarily strengthened, as if she were trying to summon enough breath to talk further, but instead she closed her eyes and sank into a coma-like sleep. Later, when Rumbochembo's helpers brought the medical supplies from the raft, I trickled quinine between her teeth. The quinine would help bring down the fever, but it was not a cure.

One by one Rumbochembo and I opened each of the medicine boxes and put the bottles in her cabinet. We worked this way for an hour or so until her cabinet was full. Then Rumbochembo left me alone. Gray shades moved down from the sky and the village fires burned brighter and the odor of smoke hung strong in the air. The chanting by now was dim, almost nonexistent. Soon the insect sounds began. I returned to Maud's side and held her tightly, my head on her chest, listening to her heartbeat and to my own dry sobs.

Night came like a black fist that punched the sun out of the sky. That first night Maud was delirious. She tossed and turned in a storm of reveries, and many moods collected in the shadows of her changing face. Sometimes she spoke African dialects and sometimes she seemed to have returned to the England of her childhood. There, bereft of the common joys of youth and along with what seemed heartrending efforts to attend to her sick mother, she tossed and turned and pined for her father's return from some distant travel. It was all there in her sweating dream state.

Through it all I watched over her and held her hand in the flickering light of an oil lamp.

The beating of drums brought me to the window. A bonfire had been built in the center of the village and the fire's red flames danced crazily into the night. The entire tribe had assembled around the fire. There were screams, chanting and the stamping of feet.

Rumbochembo stopped by, still wearing his Panama hat, and inquired about Maud. I looked him over. He was maybe twenty-five, twenty-six years old. Maud's foreman. He had told me earlier that he did all the hiring and was responsible for the general welfare of the clinic and for Maud in particular. From my short acquaintance with him, I would not have hesitated to trust him with my life.

As the drums beat fiercely, I told Rumbochembo that Maud was resting comfortably. The bonfire flames were leaping high and sending streams of sparks into the purple sky. Again more cries. What was going on? I asked.

Shango had died, Rumbochembo said. Mourners had forced pepper up the corpse's nose, to revive him, but to no avail. His body was being brought to the blaze. That's what all the shouting was about: Shango was truly dead. And that was the reason for the screams?

"That be for to find the guilty," Rumbochembo told me.

We stepped outside the hut. As much as I did not want to give my attention to Quamxandi's game at this time, there were human lives at stake and I felt an obligation to take an interest in what was going on. The gesturing, shouting Quamxandi, still dressed as a buffalo, proclaimed his bell had discovered three guilty people, a man and his two wives, the actual murderers of Shango. They stood before the witch doctor, heads bowed, their wrists tied. Next to them in the shadows of the turbulent flames stood their accomplices, five other people, also with heads bowed and wrists tied. Mutilations had taken place, but they had not produced a confession.

Quamxandi, in his infinite wisdom, raised his arms and decreed a trial. There were shouts of approval. He himself would serve as prosecutor and judge. More shouts. Quamxandi called for what Rumbochembo translated as court property or better yet, as instruments of the law. There was a brief scurrying of natives shouting orders back and forth.

In the shadowed glow of that bonfire chickens were brought forth and tied to each accomplice's wrist. Then hoods were placed over the chickens' heads and the accomplices were ordered to walk toward the fire. Rumbochembo explained: Once the hood was removed, if a chicken clucked, the person tied to it was deemed guilty. If the chicken remained silent, that person was innocent.

The assemblage howled and the bonfire leaped at the black night like a leopard at its prey. The accomplices were dragged toward the fire with the chickens tied to their wrists; three of them were seized by Quamxandi's enforcers when the chickens suddenly clucked.

Justice was swift. A woman was forced to drink sass bark poison; she ran in a circle clutching her throat, then keeled over in a fit. A man's ankles and wrists were held fast while his throat was slit. Another man was strangled and heaved bodily into the flames. The shadowed assembly stood by silently as a profusion of sparks leaped skyward.

Two of the chickens did not cluck and so two of the accused accomplices were spared. As for the original three people that Quamxandi's bell had discovered, the witch doctor ordered them brought to the river. They resisted and struggled fiercely, the man and his wives, but the many hands of justice dragged them off. At the river they would be laid on their backs, Rumbochembo said, their necks tied to stakes driven deep into the soft clay, a gift for prowling crocodiles.

It was a bloody justice I saw that night—mayhem and murder carried out in the name of the law. But as regressive as it was, it was not unique. How many times had our Western justice system falsely accused people and had them shot or beheaded or hung? But what followed that night in the Ncomi village was worse than any miscarriage of justice. In a high-pitched voice, the witch doctor blamed King Makokou for the village's ills. The king, he claimed, had provoked the terror spirit Tando by turning from the laws of the fathers, by failing to make sacrifices to appease the mighty spirit of thunder. So Makokou deserved to have his village cursed. That is what

Quamxandi proclaimed.

King Makokou was not present to defend himself. Rumbochembo explained that he was the king of many tribes and lived on a plantation a distance away. But Quamxandi's proclamation was bound to reach him nonetheless.

Angry voices were raised, arms thrown above heads. The tom-toms beat rapidly and a hectic dance started. The rumpus around the bonfire reached a fever pitch.

Then all at once Quamxandi stretched out his arms and calmed the assembly. The very flames seemed to sink lower as he spoke, every ear strained to listen. There was another reason the great sickness curse had visited the Makokou village, he said. He had learned of a legal dispute going on in Shramandazi. Shramandazi, Rumbochembo whispered to me, was a shadowy replica of this world where the dead live on as before.

Yes, he, Quamxandi, had learned that the Shramandazi courts, in order to settle this great legal dispute, were calling on the Ncomi people to give testimony. And this was why everyone was dying. They were needed as Shramandazi court witnesses.

A profound silence fell over the assembly. The bonfire's blaze lit the natives' faces.

But all was not lost, Quamxandi continued. Not yet. He, Quamxandi, would save the village from the scourge of death. Come the morning, he himself would act as an intermediary and find out what the courts needed to know from each family, and for a fee he would collect that pertinent testimony and deliver it to the Shramandazi courts himself, and thus save each family the hardship and expense of a funeral.

A soft murmur ran through the assembly.

There would be no more deaths, no more mourning, no more hardships, no more tears. He said again that his fee would be smaller than the cost of a funeral.

Didn't the Ncomi see that Quamxandi was a swindler and full of contradictions? First he blamed Shango's death on witchcraft. Then he said Tando the thunder spirit had put a curse on the village. And finally this Shramandazi farce. Didn't they see this witchcraft nonsense was merely a ploy for Quamxandi to usurp Makokou's power, just a bold move to rob the villagers of their livestock?

Rumbochembo regarded me carefully. Having been schooled by missionaries, he was Westernized to a degree. "All Ncomi know," he said, "there be sometime two, sometime three, sometime four path to one place. Most never be one path only."

"And if a family member should die after they pay their fee," I asked, "then what?"

"Then Quamxandi say dot family not give Quamxandi much good evidence and dot is why the Shramandazi court had to call them the witness themself. You sabe?"

I sabbied all right. But it still made no sense. And I was in no mood to spend much energy figuring out the ways of the Ncomi. Rumbochembo stayed with me awhile then went to sleep. I stayed on to watch the bonfire's edges turn to ashes and all the villagers return to their huts. Then I returned to the clinic to check on Maud. She seemed to be sleeping calmly.

I was tired but too restless for sleep. I thumbed through Maud's ledger. Her records were in good shape—names, dates, diseases and treatment. Years of work without recognition or reward, forgotten by the world. And for what? I asked myself what did it matter to Maud if these people, whose lives could be so easily claimed by the likes of Quamxandi, died because of disease? Was it worth sacrificing her own life for a people who were bound to face death early anyway? She had taken it as her duty. There wasn't a shred of idealism in it. But it wasn't as if she had been doing something permanently good. Her medicine, her endeavors were short-term, stop gap measures. In a few years these people in her ledger would all be dead anyway. If not by nature, then by witchcraft. I had seen three people killed outright and three others left to be ravaged by crocodiles. Why? Was it the tropics, the intense heat, the incessant rains, the white mists? Murder had nothing to do with geography, I thought. It was something that happened in the hearts of men. I lay down on an empty cot and slept until dawn.

In the morning, before the sun was fully ripe, I went to the cistern and scissored my beard with a long razor that I had dredged out from the bottom of my knapsack. I shaved with the aid of a small hand mirror I had found on Maud's table. When I returned to the hut, there was Maud, propped up in bed, her blonde hair fanned out on a pillow and her eyes bluer than I remembered. I sat next to her and held her as gently as

I could. How precious her frail body felt in my arms; how soft her downy hair behind her ears. It seemed I held her for an eternity, and when she said my name and put her arms around me, I felt as if my entire life had been justified.

To think that our two separate lives, continents apart, should now be brought together by nothing more than the sheer force of my will. It was as if I had obstructed the natural course of events, and although the rest of the world continued on its merry way, Maud and I would no longer be a part of it. So be it, I thought. Who needs the world anyway. We had each other.

Her voice was at first painfully slow—and too weak to express the emotion I had hoped for. She remembered the night before and asked me how I had found her. She seemed ashamed that I had found her in a sick condition. I told her about St. Elizabeth's and that I had been given the responsibility of delivering her medical supplies. And how long had the journey taken? I had lost so much weight. I looked so much older. As if these things mattered. And what about my schooling?

"You never wrote me," I said. "I had no way of knowing where you were."

She lowered her eyes. "Dear David," she said, "I wanted to give you every chance at your own life."

"I will never let you go again," I pledged.

She pressed her forehead against mine. She said she had heard the tom-toms in her lucid moments, and when they spoke of a white man on the river, she knew it was me. But it seemed to her to have happened a long time ago, in another life.

"I'm here now and that's all that matters." I showed her the new suit I had brought her, with the pockets and the brass buttons. "I promised you this suit seven years ago. Remember?"

"I remember," she whispered.

"Ma feel better?" asked a tired-looking Rumbochembo as he stuck his head through the entrance to the hut.

She spoke to me. "Poor fellow, he has cooked for me throughout my illness, and done my laundry, and more."

"No much bother," he said. "Mistah Collie, he be coming now. I much be glad you not be more sick."

Gradually she regained her composure and I helped her to the table. I made breakfast—first, a bowl of green tea from some leaves I'd bought from the traders at Ndjole. Then I mixed some roti flour with water and we had pancakes topped with spoonfuls of chutney. By the time we finished breakfast the sun had taken command of the sky and only the odor of ashes reminded me of horrors from the night before.

The important thing, I told her again, was that I would not be leaving her again. I would throw myself lock, stock and barrel into the life she had made in West Africa and become, like her, a healer. That is, if she would have me. I wasn't overlooking the possibility that there might have been someone else. My remark enticed a smile from her. "I loved you, Maud, from the first day I saw you," I continued.

"You were so handsome in your uniform," she said weakly.

"And so young. And yes, I loved you too."

Later that morning I met one of Maud's English-speaking companions, Claude de Castelbajac, a Belgian missionary, the man Rumbochembo called Mistah Collie. De Castelbajac and his wife Angelique ran a mission about twenty miles up river. The Belgian stopped by to check on Maud from time to time. He was an unpretentious fellow, middle-aged, shaggy haired. He smoked a pipe. After the introductions, he said he was surprised that a certain Doctor Barout had not yet dropped by.

De Castelbajac informed us that he had summoned this Barout from a field hospital about 40 kilometers away and had expected him to have visited Maud by now. I said I thought Barout should have been attending Maud the moment she showed signs of fever. The mortality rate from typhoid was very high.

But Maud was optimistic. "Bravo for Barout," she said. Then jokingly she added that her own special doctor (she meant me) had reverted back to his original vocation, that of a mailman. I didn't want Maud to know the extent of her illness and so I kept quiet. She pointed to the full medical cabinet and showed the missionary her new suit. She was so pleased, so happy at that moment, that I almost forgot myself that she was very sick. And she must have forgotten too, for when the conversation turned to Quamxandi, she informed us that as soon as she was on her feet again she would deal with him.

Toward midday, though, a tiredness caught up with her, and she drifted off to sleep. As we were leaving her hut, the

Belgian took my arm. "Only yesterday it seemed as if the end was near. But now she's in such good spirits."

"Maud has enteric fever," I said. "We are seeing the calm before the storm. Doesn't Barout know how seriously ill she is?"

"Yes, of course, but Barout has his own responsibilities. He is treating a dozen or so natives."

"The epidemic has reached his district?"

"No. The epidemic has not reached his district."

"Then why is he not here with Maud?"

De Castelbajac was silent.

I was ashamed to have made such a statement, but to have said anything else would have been a deceit. To change the subject, I told De Castelbajac the details about Shango and how Quamxandi had murdered six people. He knocked some crusty old tobacco out of his pipe, and with a face that showed no sign of surprise, he said that was the way it had been before Mademoiselle King had arrived three years ago.

In his opinion Chief Makokou was politically no match for Quamxandi. Quamxandi's power was rooted in the male members of the tribes, he said. During his exile, in fact, at a neighboring village, he had initiated a law that decreed that a man's wife must die at her husband's funeral and accompany him into the afterworld. Why is that? I asked. He said it was the only way to keep the wives from poisoning their husbands.

Surely that made sense, if you're going to play that game. Yes, I could see why King Makokou was no match for the likes of Quamxandi.

"The old order will rise again," he said thoughtfully.

King Cyprien Makokou was a heathen to the core. That's what the missionary told me. He also said that the king had graduated from a European university and spoke French, English and German. In fact, when the European powers debated the partitioning of Africa, he negotiated a treaty that made his part of the Congo a protectorate of France. "Another time, another place, Makokou might have governed a nation."

"You mean to tell me," I said, "that in one of these reed huts hangs a university sheepskin?" Maud had once said that she loved Africa because it was full of surprises. King Makokou was certainly a surprise to me.

The Belgian laughed. "A lot that counts for out here."

That afternoon, while Maud slept and Claude and I talked, the missionary suddenly sprang to his feet and bowed. Behind me, the king himself—I had no doubt it was him—appeared in the doorway like a splash of sunlight, unannounced and in all his glory. Tall, muscular, broad-faced with skin as smooth as black velvet, he wore a leopard skin headdress, a loincloth and a necklace made up of long teeth. He looked to be about fifty. With him were three spear-carrying subordinates with two large dogs on bush rope leashes. The king entered the hut and his followers stayed outside.

I was introduced as a friend of Mademoiselle King, the bearer of medicine by way of London.

"A noble gesture indeed," said the king. He sat and bid us to do the same. A profound sadness fell over the chief's face. "Ma is truly magnificent. I am much grieved by her sickness.

And today, how is she?" You could hear the pathos of Africa in his deep, resonant voice.

"There's hope," I said, and I offered him my condolences on Shango's passing."

"Save your grief, Mister Unger," said the king, "My father sired a hundred and twenty sons. Shango was among the oldest."

A wise and gentle man, that's what De Castelbajac had called Makokou. Concerning the butchery of the night before, the sighing king said it truly dismayed him, but he admitted to being powerless against witchcraft.

Through the doorway I could see that the tribesmen had gathered into a compact group, black and shimmering in the sun's glare, ready to lay their fishing spears, their chickens and furniture at Quamxandi's feet. It was such a swindle— Tando's revenge and the Shramandazi court dispute. It riled me to see the witch doctor getting away with it.

One word led to another and the missionary let on that even Maud's medicine was regarded by the tribesmen as a form of magic. It certainly did nothing to eradicate witchcraft. On hearing De Castelbajac's words, King Makokou drew a deep breath and rolled his eyes. De Castelbajac had stepped on the king's toes. After all, it was at the king's behest that Maud had brought her European medicine to his village.

The king stood up abruptly. "Let us go outside," he said, lifting his arm.

De Castelbajac and I left the hut on the heels of the king. His guardsmen and dogs kept their distance. A strong afternoon light had settled on the lofty crowns of the tall trees in the forest beyond the huts. Chattering squads of flying monkeys, using their tails as rudders, tiptoed across a vast garden of orchids and ferns that hung from the underside of limbs. The beauty of the jungle was so great, so much in contrast to the sickness and suffering of the Ncomi tribe.

King Makokou led the way, walking briskly while circumventing the desolate lines of villagers with their offerings. "My friend here," the chief said addressing me as I walked at his side, "believes my village is in this wretched state because I won't allow him to preach his God, a God, mind you, who relies on Fleet Street publishers to deliver his word. Ha!" I detected a hint of an old, rehashed argument between the Belgian and the king.

"Monsieur De Castelbajac," he said then, turning to the missionary, "your bible is a wise book, but you must know it's a bronze age production. Do you really think it's an escape hatch to the outside of all this?" He made a circular motion with his arm as if to include not only the observable jungle but the world at large. Having said as much, the chief lifted his palms upward, and with an imprecating smile, declared: "Your God, my friend, is an idea, and no matter how fervently you believe in that idea, it will not take you outside yourself. Never." His smile turned wiser. "All ideas—yours, mine—are inside the head, on this side of the wall. You agree, no?"

"Mystics have seen beyond the wall," said the missionary meekly with a side glance.

"Mystics, you say?" The king laughed broadly, as perhaps

only a king can. "And why not throw in a few martyrs while you are at it."

De Castelbajac came back to press the issue. "There is a spiritual element that takes us beyond your wall." Unlike the king, he was a man of few words.

A brief snort interrupted the king's fragile solemnity. "The spiritual; you make it sound like something on rental from your God."

Spreading his regal arms, allowing his leopard skin to hang wing-like at his side, the king spoke again: "My dear friend," he chided, "the spiritual is man's crowning achievement. Is it not? What man adds to nature, what he adds to those mountains of matter ruled by immutable laws that would have existed even if man had not emerged from the dust. Isn't that the way it is?"

He looked me square in the eye, inviting me to see his point of view. I had the notion that he liked to hear himself talk. Nevertheless, his charcoal hair under his leopard headdress wasn't specked with gray for nothing. He was a wise old coot. "Tools, civilization, are they not part of the spiritualization of matter?" he asked. "Works of the imagination seeking to escape their anchor in the dumb rock of matter? That's what the spirit is. Yes, or no?"

He paused, inviting my assent. For my part, I had to go along. The desolate huts were now a long distance away. The missionary remained a thoughtful listener. Having taken us this far, the king's deep, dark eyes caught a shaft of the flaming sun and his voice rang once more. "Tell me, aren't the makers of music, the poets, the engineers, aren't they the true spiritualists? Aren't they the true explorers of that realm beyond matter? Are they not? They reach out, they soar, they add to man's spiritual bank account. Don't you agree?"

I wasn't too sure at this point. Pausing, the king tapped his forehead. "But the all-too-human brain, it holds man hostage, trapped in the very flesh and blood of matter. We are each of us tied to this earth, imprisoned."

I agreed. I was starting to see what he meant. I was impressed. The missionary wasn't. "God makes us see whatever He wants us to see," De Castelbajac said guardedly.

Makokou acknowledged this with a sweeping bow, and a flash of yellow teeth, but refused to be put off. It was evident that he was talking of something close to his heart. Our path led to a cooler, shaded area of the jungle, and he followed the zigzag flight of a squad of butterflies, each the size of two of his joined hands. "The spiritual is born of sorrow. The human soul is soaked in sorrow."

I wasn't exactly certain what he was talking about, but I sensed what he meant. Makokou gestured in the direction of a fleet of monkeys swinging from one high tree to another. They suffered, he said, matter-of-factly, the monkeys did, as did other jungle creatures. Yes, they became ill; they were tormented by predators, no doubt about it, but sorrow was not their lot. No, it was not. And did we know why?

Again De Castelbajac fell under the king's melancholy gaze. "Because sorrow," the king said, "is the noblest of emotions and reserved for man; it is at the very heart of man's creativity, the height of his crowning reason, his soul's very lifeblood. Yes, it is. Sorrow."

I felt the awful weight of Makokou's words.

Grief and anger were great thought provokers, he said, but sorrow was the mother of the human intellect. Sorrow. Only noble sorrow. How he rolled his large eyes when he spoke. Sorrow, he continued, sparked the imagination into being, and made man's vision clear. Sorrow. It inspired the higher forms of thought. Yes, it did. For out of an infinite sorrow man explored nature, wasn't that right? And in so doing, he imaginatively ascended into the spiritual realm. Sorrow.

He spoke without emotion, as if stating a bald irrepressible fact. I listened, and the very jungle, its rooted trees and vines, its blossoming flowers, seemed to heed the king's ancient wisdom.

We continued circling the village and Makokou rolled his eyes skyward. A Great Chaos existed at the heart of the universe, he explained. A Great Latency, a Great Spiritual Reservoir. He said it comprised all the jumbled laws and disordered principles of nature, and dealt with every possible human design, aspiration, accident or chance possibility.

And in the face of this Great Chaos, he declared, man's vaulted freedom was but a puny whisper, for no dose of human thought or action could encompass this Great Chaos; it could only discover more and more of it, the Great uncreated spirituality of the universe.

Oh, how man sought to understand this complete Godhead truth, he said, so that all of creation would have no secrets from him. "Ye shall be as gods," he laughed boisterously. "But in vain, Mister Unger!" He turned to De Castelbajac. "Imagine, a Promethean monster straining to rival its master. O dear Lord, God forbid!" His coarse, earthy laughter was truly Rabelaisean.

The king may have been in great form that day, I don't know, but the missionary was not in his league. However, he did manage to make a point. "You said before that the laws of the universe would exist even if man did not exist. And where would those laws have existed if not in the mind of God?"

The king placed a brotherly palm on the missionary's shoulder. "You are right, my friend. But such a God is not the God of your Fleet Street publishers..." (He glanced my way but continued to address the missionary) "...who need man to complete His grand design. The God you refer to is the Ncomi God, Anzambe, the Indifferent One, the thinking man's God. Don't you agree?"

The missionary's deadpan demeanor suggested he did not. The king's own face expressed a serious turn of mind. At this point I threw in my two cents. "King Makokou," I said, "Quamxandi is fleecing your villagers on a grand scale. Why don't you stop him?"

"Quamxandi? Stop him? How?"

"You could tie his hands and feet and ship him down the river. The crocs will do the rest."

The king's eyes grew large. "Dispose of him? Are you saying I should have him killed?"

He was patronizing me. "You'd all be better off," I said.

"But I would never do that, Mister Unger. No, no, no. And you know why? Because Quamxandi's family paid a lot of money to make him a witch doctor. He holds a very exalted office. He is the official manager of malevolent spirits. He belongs to a cult as old as Africa itself. Besides, as one of you Europeans once said: 'Beware that in casting out your devil you cast out the best thing in you.' That is how I feel about Quamxandi."

I couldn't buy what the king was saying. "In deference to your majesty's wisdom, I still can't see any good coming from this fellow. Just do away with him, I say. He's a bad apple."

"Yes, Quamxandi is a very bad apple. But he has a right to live. The child of darkness is a brother to the child of light. How can we forget that? Once upon a time you Europeans gave lip service to a big idea, that of original sin, remember? Now you are bent on perfecting man. Another big idea. Hogwash, all of it. We Africans suffer no such illusions. All societies, my dear Mister Unger, are top heavy with power-hungry Calibans. We know that. But as for banishing Quamxandi, we have no right."

"He's evil," I insisted. "You should fight him."

"And what has fighting evil gotten you Europeans? Whenever you have tried to banish it you have only driven it underground. Your Age of Reason gave birth to a Reign of Terror, did it not? We Africans have our witchcraft and our human sacrifices, but compared to your large-scale wars... Please, Mister Unger, people in glass houses, you know..."

What more could I say? I knew when I was outclassed.

Chapter Nine

That night Maud King was in a bad state—with lots of abdominal pain and sweat, and, again, delirium. Her skin, her eyes, her hair became ashy and lifeless. The bacteria had attacked her digestive system. I told De Castelbajac I had to operate, to repair the damage done to her intestines. He insisted Doctor Barout would arrive by the next morning. I told him I had waited too long already, that Rumbochembo would assist me. I walked with him across the village toward the river. He would stay, he said, if I wanted him to. No, I said, his wife was alone and waiting for him.

His final words were that I should not give up on Barout, and that he himself would be back in the morning. I waved; he hopped in his canoe and left. The moon glowed pale high above the surrounding rosewood and walnut trees. An unbroken chatter came from the black forest wall, more of a hiss actually, as if the universe had sprung a leak. I walked back to the village feeling weak, empty and small, powerless, at the mercy of malevolent forces. As I re-entered the village, I heard that familiar chant once more. It grew louder, more insistent. Only this time it wasn't Shango that was being called. Rather it was, "Ma! Ma! Ma!"

Quamxandi's horned buffalo head came bobbing in the moonlight, and behind him, out of the shadowy night, his infernal squad of mourners.

They sensed Maud's hour was near and they were entreating her soul not to leave her body. Just as he had done with Shango, Quamxandi, with his high-stepping dance, led the mourners. Then he turned, saw me, and for a moment he stopped. Then, more defiantly and louder than before, he cried out, "Ma! Ma! Ma!" The mourners, chalky white, bent at the waist, their hands near the ground, followed him as he moved in the direction of Maud's hut. "Ma! Ma! Ma!" He was taunting me, telling me that my medicine was useless against the terror of Tando.

I'd had enough. I ran across the village toward Maud's hut with the mourners' chants and Quamxandi's taunting cries following behind me. Once at the hut, I reached inside the doorway and found the cold steel of my Martini-Henry's barrel. After the wholesale slaughter of the night before, I didn't want that crazy witch doctor anywhere near Maud. Not him, his bell or his mourners. I would kill him first.

I cranked my carbine, ran out from the hut and shouted at Quamxandi to stay away, that I'd blast his head off if he took another step. I was angry enough to pull the trigger and I guess it showed. The witch doctor crouched low and slowly backed off. He wasn't about to challenge a loaded carbine. His mourners continued chanting, but lower and lower, as they too dissolved in the darkness of the night.

The sound of running feet is what I heard next, and from

the darkness behind me Rumbochembo emerged, holding a lantern. I figured he would tell me that I would bring "much too bad trouble" by causing Quamxandi to lose face in front of his people. But I didn't care. Maud was dying, physically melting away in the terrible grip of typhoid, but her spirit was alive, a magnificent, victorious element of her being. Quamxandi's presence would be the death of her spirit. It would mean his witchcraft had prevailed, after all. I couldn't allow that to happen.

If Maud had to die, then better she left with the illusion of having done some permanent good. I wanted her to believe that she had been victorious and not wasted her time with this clinic of hers.

Rumbochembo shook my arm, as if to awaken some slumber in my soul. "Ma be bad sick!" His voice was choked and the lantern trembled in his hand.

We hurried back to the hut. There in the shadowy gloom, Maud was stretched out in pain, forlorn, but conscious. I felt myself in the grip of a kind of inertia. There was a yellow glow in her eyes. The bacteria had invaded her liver. I had waited too long. I quickly set up as many lamp poles as I could find and Rumbochembo made a small fire, placed upon it a small pan of water, and boiled every available surgical instrument—a razor blade, shears, forceps, needles, catgut ligatures... everything except the scalpel. Boiling water would blunt the scalpel's cutting edge, so once the sterile instruments were put aside, I added a strong formaldehyde solution to the boiling water and a drop of methanol, put on a pair of hospital gloves, and with the forceps, suspended the scalpel over the solution's steamy vapors.

Next I poured a cup of linseed oil into a second pan and placed it over the same fire. While the linseed oil heated, I prepared a potion of bella donna, a bitter crystalline, dabbed a piece of cotton into it and asked Maud to inhale the potion. This would limit the excretion of mucus in her air passages during the operation. Rumbochembo then heated a silver spatula directly over our small fire. Having attended lectures on modern antiseptics at King's College Hospital in London, I felt very confident. The liver, I knew, had a good chance of recovering, but not the intestine. My chief worry beyond the operation itself was her heart. If it mutinied, there was nothing I could do.

Now in the pan that contained the hot linseed oil I added carbolic acid and put that aside too.

Maud inhaled the bella donna and her eyes became glassy, her hairline dark with dampness. Her cheeks were painfully hollow. Gradually her pupils dilated. "Patch me up, Davey," she said. "You can do it." Her hands and legs shook uncontrollably. She was very weak, her pulse quick but feeble.

Rumbochembo and I lifted her onto a table and I prepared a shot of morphine to calm her. "Remember the night of the scorpion?" she said. "You did a magnificent job then. Remember?"

"I'll do an even better job this time," I promised.

She drew me to her and smiled. "You better. I'll haunt you if you don't."

She kissed the palm of my hand. Her humor was the very soul of her and had allowed her to survive the harsh jungle's despair. I spread out my instruments and injected her with morphine. She lay straight back on the table and her spasms subsided.

"Now breathe deeply," I said and carefully placed a wad of gauze soaked in ether over her nose and mouth. When she lost consciousness, I removed her undergarments, shaved her abdomen and painted it with a solution of picric acid and iodine. Poor Rumbochembo; her faithful "number one mon" could not bear to look and turned his face aside.

With as steady a hand as I could manage, I made the first incision, a vertical cut from her navel down to her groin area, careful not to cut too deep or I would have injured her transverse colon. Once that first cut was made, my hand became steady and I felt in total control. I cauterized the bleeding with the hot spatula. That done, I made the second incision, a horizontal cut across the top of the vertical one, so that the two cuts formed a T. Again I cauterized the bleeding and folded back the abdominal flesh into a perfect V with the entire intestinal system exposed, a tight, winding arrangement of convoluted tubes, four sections of which were perforated by the virulent enteric bacteria. She had periosteal lesions in the cecum area of the large intestine just above her appendix, another lesion around the ileocaecal valve. There was a jagged ulceration in the middle ileum region of her small intestine, and a fourth inflammation on her right side, in the transverse colon itself.

My shears lifted the diseased bowel parts and I cut three inches off the end of each infected portion and sutured those sections to the remaining healthy intestinal tube. Then I drenched a cloth in the carbolic-linseed solution with the forceps until it became putty-like. And I inserted the cloth on the patched intestines. Once the substance adhered to the sewn joints, I removed the cloth. Maud was now antiseptically clean and in no danger of microorganisms re-infecting the region.

There was nothing more I could do. Again threading the catgut ligature, I neatly closed her abdomen. I had worked on her more than three hours and had done as fine a job as any seasoned doctor might have. I'll never believe otherwise.

I was alone in the room when Maud regained consciousness. It was about three in the morning. The lantern light was dim, but even so, when she awoke what I saw was a remarkable transformation: Her eyes were clear and bright; her hair was no longer ashy but a beautiful rose color and her skin had the fresh blush of a young girl. It was macabre in a way. It was as though the typhoid, having made its point, was allowing her to enjoy a final bloom, a moment's respite before it would finish its work.

I propped her up a bit. "How did it go, Davey?" She managed a wisp of a smile despite her forced breathing.

"It went fine." Her forehead was moist to the touch of my lips.

"There's not much time, Davey." Her eyes narrowed, she

pressed her hand to her heart. "It's weak." Her tone was serious. She was near death and she knew it and she wanted me to know it too.

I had made a decision during the night. "When Claude returns," I said resolutely, "I'm going to ask him to marry us. That is, if you'll have me."

"You are the soul of kindness," she said, her eyes moist, her breathing laborious and uneven. "We've lived together, you and I, and we've lived apart, but I suppose we have never been separated."

The lantern's glow lent her face a wondrous sheen. It was so smooth, her face, as smooth as a stone that had been washed at the edge of the sea for a thousand years. I had to marvel at her. "You know," she said, "the other day I was thinking of these last few years. Here at the clinic. Remember that poem you read at my house, that silly small poem about a person who after an adventurous life is urged to return home?"

"'Creep home and find your place there, the spent and maimed among...'"

"Remember you asked me if I'd ever return to England and I said my real home was elsewhere? I thought of that poem the other day, and I said to myself, here I am in the middle of Africa, my real home, and certainly among the spent and maimed. And you remember how it ends, that poem? It ends, 'God grant you find one face there you loved when all was young.' And I thought of you, David, my Saturday mailman who gave me such great comfort, and who finally brought me all the love I've ever needed. 'God grant you find one face there you loved when all was young.'"

She pressed my hand to her cheekbone. "You've made me so very happy."

We talked for the next few hours and agreed that death is only a phase of life and that the shared moment lives forever. In our silences I experienced a profound sense of acceptance and serenity.

I held Maud to me, and felt the shadow of our passing souls as they crossed one into the other, so that we became a single entity.

Maud never saw the first hint of dawn when it entered the room. I kissed her forehead and closed her eyes.

Later that morning I dressed Maud in the outfit I had brought from Douala. Rumbochembo, meanwhile, fashioned a rough coffin from the wood of the medical supplies crates. Together we placed her inside. Then we carried her to a shaded place under a tree and lowered her in the grave that Rumbochembo's men had prepared.

It was a beautiful service. Except for Quamxandi, who was nowhere to be seen, the entire village attended, the maimed and the healthy alike. Even tribes people from other villages came to Maud's funeral, and some, dressed in batik cloth, sang in the language of the Baoule, "Laagoh budji gnia." Lord, it is you who has made all.

De Castelbajac stood at the head of the grave where the dug-out earth had not been piled and said no one but a saint would find her duty in easing the pain of others, even at the cost of her own life. Then under a sun that had rolled across the sky like a brass coin, he read from his book, the one that the king had said was a bronze age production—as well as a product of London's Fleet Street. He read from that book and then closed it.

King Makokou too spoke with a heavy heart on what Miss King had meant to the Ncomi people. "She found us broken and made us whole. She restored our faith in ourselves." Then the missionary's wife, Angelique, demure and reticent and dressed in white, sang a hymn in a beautiful voice that seemed to render the service even sadder than it already was. "Lord, in Thee is all our trust," she sang. I thought of what Makokou had said about sorrow and I thought perhaps beauty too was wrapped in sadness. Perhaps.

When Angelique finished her hymn, Rumbochembo directed three of his men to fill in the grave. I waited until the very end, until everyone had left and there was nothing more to wait for, and then I left too.

The world looked no different now that Maud was dead. The same dark trees stood in the forest, making a long straight line across an indifferent sky; the same dull smoke curled out of the bubbling kettles; the tall grass still swayed when reached by a breeze; the crickets still whirred; nothing had changed. The world did not notice that Maud King was gone.

I reflected on Quamxandi's absence and saw that he had lost face in front of his own people. He had retreated to the jungle to lick his wounds, I thought. Or else he had made his journey to Shramandazi to carry out his mandate. Either way I was glad to be rid of him.

I found myself in the clinic sometime later, though I had been so lost in thought that I did not remember going there. I simply found myself there, with Rumbochembo, the king, and De Castelbajac. We sat at the table and drank Maud's palm toddy. And it was a damn good toddy too, strong but not bitter or sappy. I had found an old cadet uniform of mine among Maud's possessions and I gave it to Rumbochembo. He loved it, especially the hat, and thanked me profusely.

When the chief's dogs started barking—they were stationed outside our hut—we looked out and saw four tribesmen emerge from the forest. Or at least we saw their bobbing heads above the tall grass that separated the village from the forest. On their shoulders were long sagging poles bearing a weight. We couldn't see what they were carrying until they entered a clearing where the grass was matted down. Then a white man lazily rolled out of a hammock. The weary carriers sat on the ground and passed a jug. Rumbochembo said they stayed far from the huts because they would not want to mix with a tribe that had fallen under the evil spell.

The white man, though, he headed straight toward us, stiff, unsteady, with a satchel swinging at his side. He came wobbling across the center of the village in a green tunic and boots, sweat rings under his arms, epaulets on his shoulders. I'll never forget him, an overfed, swollen fellow he was, and he took his sweet time, occasionally slapping his neck at mosquitoes. De Castelbajac said it was Barout.

Finally he stood at the doorway, out of breath and mopping his brow with a handkerchief. He ignored Rumbochembo, who was squatting there, and regarded Makokou and myself with a jaundiced eye. His attention shifted to De Castelbajac. With a heavy slur (he spoke a choppy French), he said, "Well, where is she? The English lady that you called me for? The sick one." The odor of cognac was heavy on his breath. His face was starchy and pockmarked. His nose had an uncommonly sharp point to it. He looked for a place to drop his satchel. His hands were shaky.

There was a long silence. Then the missionary told the drunken fool that he was no longer needed, that we had expected him a week ago. It was too late. Mademoiselle King had died early in the morning.

"What?" cried Barout. Slowly he rotated his head, looking at each of us, as if trying to decide who had spoken. "Who died? The patient?" His twisted mouth hung open and it took him a full minute to understand what he'd been told. In that minute who knows what incriminations he discarded, what rationales he tossed off.

"She was in the advanced stages of enteric fever," I said. "I operated on her."

He squinted at me. His eyes were colorless. His nose bent like a nail hit the wrong way, his mouth like a twisted rope. "You operated?" he asked, a livid anger rising in his eyes.

"He's a medical student," said the missionary stoutly.

"A student? A student?" Barout moved toward the missionary and his arms flayed the air. "A student is not a doctor! A student should know not to meddle!"

If he had a club, I believe, he would have struck the missionary for trying to defend me. His scorn filled the room. "I could have saved her," he said harshly. He looked around, as if to see where she might be, as if he might still bring her back. Then he pointed an angry, threatening finger at me. "You had no authority. You should have waited for me!" His nose grew sharper. "You idiot, you will answer for this in a court of law!"

I came to my feet. I couldn't care two hoots for his court of law and I was determined to tell him that.

"Sit down," Barout demanded.

I sprang and caught him by the collar and landed a hard right to his jaw. Rumbochembo quickly pulled me off him or I might have done permanent damage to the drunken lout. The next thing I knew, he was running from me, stumbling, shouting, his mouth spitting blood, running across the open space in the center of the village.

The tribesmen and their families poured out of their huts to witness the goings on. As soon as I felt Rumbochembo ease up his hold on me, I broke from him and went after Barout. What a sight it must have been, one white man chasing another while Makokou's dogs barked and Rumbochembo and others shouted.

Eventually I slowed down. Unless he stumbled, I would not catch him; he was too far ahead of me. I had only the fact that he was still holding his jaw to satisfy me. He reached his destination and summoned his weary carriers to him. Then they waded off through the high grass and exited the village by forcing an opening in the sapling fence. I counted myself lucky to be rid of him.

My companions, though, were still shouting. Why? What were they trying to tell me? With the dogs barking and the distance between us, I couldn't hear what they were trying to say.

I was still on the near side of the tall grass, and I would have seen what was about to happen if I had turned in time. We never see the entire picture. That's what Makokou meant. We can only experience ourselves and nothing outside of that. I had no reason to turn. If I had, I'd have seen the leopard moving up on me and then crouching flat on its belly in the tall grass ready to lunge.

When it sprang I was hit with its full weight and dragged to the ground. In the dust I struggled for my life. I can't say at what point I realized that I was battling a man, a powerful man—Quamxandi in all his imperial fury. He had me down on my back, under him, and with the leopard fist of his left hand at my throat, he reached for my face with his other clawed fist.

I was no match for his terrible strength. I held his wrist and tried to bring up my knees. But he forced his knee into my chest, and suddenly Rumbochembo's warning came back to me: "Him want you eyes!"

"No!" I cried out. "No!"

But it was clear to me that's exactly what he wanted. In his crazy witchcraft world, the eyes of a white man were precious.

They held the white man's power. They were more valuable even than the white flesh, which was sold on the coast by secret societies in those days. And moreover, my eyeballs in his possession would redeem him in front of his people, show them that although I had insulted him, he was my superior. His clawed fist trembled before my eyes. His black face strained. I had his right wrist in my grip but couldn't hold him back. His filthy leopard claw inched closer. I felt myself weakening.

The claw dug into my eyebrow. I could hear the tribesmen calling his name in the distance. He was already being hailed. A trickle of blood entered my eye from where his claw had torn my brow. His black face poured sweat; his black eyes shone with ecstasy.

I was so focused on keeping his claw from my eye that when the shot rang out I didn't quite connect it to the fact that his hold on my neck instantly tightened tenfold, beyond human power, it seemed. Then just as suddenly it loosened. I had heard the roar but I failed to connect it to the fact that he had been shot. Nor did he, not immediately. He still bore down on me with all his weight and it took several seconds for him to know that a bullet had gone through him. Then it flashed across his face, the shock of recognition that a vital organ had been hit and he was dying. It registered in the pupils of his eyes, the way they froze, and it was confirmed in the quick flutter of his heavy eyelids. The knowledge of death, that's what hit him. Not only the bullet but what the bullet brought. Death. He had thought himself exempt from death.

With a final breath he fell headlong on top of me, his clawed fist simply scratching my forehead. I quickly got out from under him and the dark heart blood that oozed from his chest.

It had happened fast. I had made him lose face before his people and he had attacked me. The villagers had seen it, had cheered him on, but now they were quiet. The shouting had stopped. Makokou's dogs still barked, but no one came out to see if Quamxandi were alive or dead. As far as the villagers were concerned, the fatal shot might have come from some supernatural realm of the spirits, beyond mortal control, something that had to be and that no human could interfere with it. It was ordained.

I gave Quamxandi one last look, then got myself up out of the dust and started back to the clinic. It was strange. I still expected a commotion to erupt. After all, a witch doctor had just been killed. But there was no sound beyond the barking dogs. My companions, the three of them, stood at the hut entrance and waited for me. I walked toward them slowly, still in a daze, wondering who had fired the shot. The trees were motionless; not a leaf stirred. The vultures in the high branches stood as still as statues. I could feel the eyes of the village men as I passed the high mound of ashes where the bonfire had been.

A tiny wisp of smoke still hung over the clinic window. It was only a bare thread of smoke, but enough to tell me where the shot had been fired from. Someone in the clinic had picked up my carbine, placed it on the windowsill, drawn a bead on Quamxandi and pulled the trigger. Either

Rumbochembo, Makokou, or De Castelbajac. One of them.

Someone behind me shouted, "Tando!" "Tando!" another voice called out. Then the name Tando was repeated, loudly at first, then lower and lower, until it became a chant.

It took me a moment to realize what was happening. The villagers thought that Tando the thunder spirit had struck down Quamxandi, that the loudness of my carbine was the noise of Tando's thunder. Well, let it be, I thought. Let it be. As I continued toward the clinic, a group of female mourners was already moving on their hands and knees toward where Quamxandi lay. The three men stopped talking as I approached the door and we all went in.

"Are you all right?" De Castelbajac asked anxiously. The cut across my brow looked worse than it actually was.

"He's dead," I said.

Rumbochembo handed me a cup of water. As I drank, King Makokou watched me, shaking his head from side to side. I finished the water and put down the cup.

"To whom do I owe my thanks?" I said.

As if I might discern the truth merely by looking at them, they each diverted their eyes.

"Well?" I asked.

"No be right for you to know," said Rumbochembo finally.

Okay, so I wasn't to know. For my own good, I supposed; in case I was caught later and forced to talk, tortured, what have you, it was better I didn't know. They were each taking the credit, or maybe the blame, depending on how you looked at it. A snicker passed between the king and De Castelbajac.

"What's that?" I asked, reaching for a rag to wipe the blood from my brow.

The king softly muttered, "Didn't you hear? Tando has disposed of Quamxandi."

"Best way for you to be gone," said Rumbochembo. "No much good for you to be here. They come take you in big numbers." He meant, of course, that Barout would have his military police after me in no time and there was no point in hanging around.

That evening, after a long ceremony of good-byes, I left. The raft that carried me to the Ncomi village took me away. I had come alone and alone I left. The next morning the tom-toms started beating. Their message was that white men, soldiers, were coming up the river. Barout had reached the Belgian authorities and they had dispatched their soldiers to arrest me, and so I headed my raft ever deeper into the interior.

For months on end I trekked through jungles and was sheltered by tribes that knew I had opposed the Belgian authorities. The Belgians, it seemed, had put a price on my head. But the Belgian state had treated the natives badly, especially those in the rubber and ivory producing regions. And so instead of turning me in, the tribes offered me protection. To the chiefs I was known as "mtu mzuri," a good person.

When the wet season came I again moved down the swollen waterways. I traveled south to the villages of Ewo and Okoyo and in time reached the coast by little known rivers. At Pointe Noire I landed a job in the fire room of a French freighter, and to escape the gloom and heat below, at night I slept on the deck under the stars.

Africa was full of mysteries. The matter of who shot Quamxandi sometimes crossed my mind. I thought of Quamxandi, and I thought of Monsieur Dupre, the French trader. Had he faked his insanity and absconded with that horde of exotic pelts? Or had he really fancied himself his own executioner and shot himself? And if that was the case, why hadn't we found his body? And I thought, unceasingly, of Maud King.

I finally ended up back in England, but I did not finish medical school. A student I could not continue to be. But I did call on a few of my old friends, including my former supervisor, the Scotsman, at St. Elizabeth's Hospital in London. I told him about Maud King's demise. From him, I suppose, all of Britain learned that Maud King had died. The press handled it with high solemnity. Dignitaries wrote to the London *Times* and her obituary was filled with anecdotes. For a while the entire Maud King mystique was revived. Kipling himself dedicated a poem to her memory. When I called on my old landlady at Cambridge, she said that certain government officials had been looking for me concerning Maud King.

The government dispatched some naval personnel to Makokou. The papers reported that they recovered Maud's body and buried her again at sea, with full military honors. She had never sought such honors, of course, and they likely would not have pleased her.

My life continued, but it was an unfocused affair at best,

desultory at times, and I drifted about for a good number of years. Now and then I shipped out to sea, mostly for the purpose of trading in gems. It seemed an adequate diversion.

Once, during a conversation with a sea captain, Rumbochembo's name came up. The captain told me he knew of him. We were sure it was the same Rumbochembo because of the old naval cadet hat my companion told me he wore, the one I had given him. He was a prosperous trader in the Douala area, the captain said. Quite prosperous, in fact, and he had all the trappings to prove it—a sturdy pair of English boots, a couple more gold teeth than when I had known him, and a slew of wives, six or seven of them, as the captain recalled, a wife at each of his main trading posts. I was happy for him.

As for Claude De Castelbajac, I dropped him several postcards in care of his Congo station on the chance that he might still be there. I received no answer. Then years later, as if my cards had reached their destination all at once, Angelique, Claude's wife, wrote me in care of my London flat that Claude was in a French hospital. He had volunteered as a chaplain in the French army and he had been gassed on the western front. I wasn't surprised.

A few years later I visited my old stretcher-bearer friend Bapu. I was in India at the time trading gems and Bapu had become quite the public figure. He had been proclaimed the Mahatma, the Great Soul. But he'd been accused of attempting to overthrow the British government, so I had to visit him in jail. He wore a shawl and was suffering with a bad appendix.

He remembered me well, and he expressed his sorrow at the passing of Maud King. "A fine woman," he said. "When I read of Miss King in the paper, I thought of you and the time we had together. In Natal, with our ambulances. We had given you up for good that time in the Nogoma Valley." He smiled.

I smiled too. "A stretcher bearer goes where the action is."

Following a silence, he said. "She is still a part of your life, your Miss King, I can see that."

"She will always be a part of my life. And so will you, Bapu."

"David, drop by again," he said when I was leaving. "You will know where to find me," he added, referring to the fact that the British were always putting him in jail. "It is always good to see an old friend. It tells me the world has not changed that much."

Life goes on, the years go by. There are times we return to the past, as with my visiting Bapu in jail, and there are times the opposite happens, when the past catches up to us. One Sunday in the south of France the past did just that to me. I had gone to the city of Nice for the climate mostly, but there I found a city given to carnival festivities and so I stayed and worked the cabarets for a while as a magician.

One Sunday, at the swanky Casino Club, I was at the roulette wheel when I heard myself addressed by a deep and melodious voice, a voice I never thought I'd hear again.

"Why, as I live and breathe, Mister David Unger. It is such a pleasure to see you."

I turned to see King Makokou. I grasped his large hand and he gave me a brotherly hug. Decked out in a tailored hounds tooth suit from Savile Row, topped off with a straw boater, he looked more regal among Europeans than he did when I knew him in Africa. He had to be near seventy, but his eyes were as bright as ever, his basso voice just as resonant. He had lived abroad for some years, he told me, but he planned to return to his homeland. Was he travelling alone? No, he was with his aunt and his newest wife, a mere child of twenty. They had been shopping in Paris. Would I care to join him for dinner? I was delighted.

I certainly enjoyed the king's company that evening. It was so good to see an old friend. He was not surprised I had never married. To have loved and been loved by Maud King put an end to all other women, I told him. That was not his way, he said, but he understood. I mentioned that De Castelbajac had been gassed in the war and that Rumbochembo had become a trader. He knew about Rumbochembo but was dismayed that Europe had not been so kind to his old missionary friend. When our dinner was completed I couldn't resist one request. It had been many years since we had last seen each other.

"With your kind permission, your royalty, I'd like to ask you a question."

The king smiled broadly. "Mister Unger, you need not stand on ceremony with me."

I struggled for a way to begin, but before I could do so, the king saved me the trouble. " I did it," he said. He finished his wine. "That was your question, was it not? Which of us shot the witch doctor?"

So, he had done it. "Why?" I asked. "Why did you do it? You seemed the least likely to have done such a thing after that argument we had. Remember? You lectured me about how good and evil were brothers and every society had its Calibans. You said Quamxandi represented the underside of life and that it was futile to repress him. You do remember that, don't you?"

"Yes, of course I remember," he said.

"Then why?"

"Because, Mister Unger, Quamxandi was my responsibility. And just as I had to protect him from you, I also had to protect you from him. You were a guest in my village and Quamxandi had no right to treat you as he did. He showed bad manners."

I tried not to laugh but couldn't help it. "Bad manners?"

"Yes, witchcraft I could abide, but not..."

"Bad manners."

The king bowed. "Precisely."

I signaled the waiter to bring our check and put my arm on Makokou's shoulder and kept him from reaching for his wallet. "If you'll allow me, your royalty, I'd like to do the honors."

"The least you can do." He laughed boldly, as perhaps only a king can.

I continued in my original profession after that trip, as an entertainer. For many years I mystified audiences in the coastal cafes around the world with my magic. Then one day

I ended up on the very edge of civilization, at Tierra del Fuego, near the South America horn.

There I met a man called Willard Meilstrup. He was a deep sea oil driller. He came with his ship to that treeless land of hawks and owls and Mesozoic mountains; he came to a land of howling Antarctic winds and tortuous channels, in search of oil. He was a man of many talents, many pursuits, a promoter of sporting events especially, an impresario—so many things. He was also a partner in a circus, and one evening he found me entertaining in a waterfront dive. I sang, I danced, I took chances with my magic that only a magician with nothing to lose would take. He liked what he saw, and right there he hired me as a magician for his circus. In time, through a fortuitous turn of events, I became the circus master of ceremonies and have held that post ever since.

I give the world its due in return for a place to lay my head. I sing, I dance, I don my silk top hat and twirl my silver cane and use what skill I have with my repertoire of illusions. But a man is more than he appears. I am not only the silvery glitter in the spotlight and not only the music that soft-shoes across the tanbark floor.

When the shades of night fall and my performance is over and the clowns depart and the animals are led to their stalls and the empty tent lights put out and it is time for my head to find a pillow, we are together again, Maud and I. Whether in the heart of a city or out somewhere in a rural village, we relive the days we spent in each other's company. We go traipsing through the hills of the Bakoki people, her camera strapped to her shoulder and her specimen bottles and net in hand. Over and over again, we huddle under a giant mushroom during a thunderstorm and she hands that beggar Bokomo a Victoria coin and tells him to give it to his Obo to let him back in the village. And we ponder his laughter in the distance.

I see her. I hear her and I wind her in my arms as I always have. And her face is as smooth as a stone that has been washed at the edge of the sea for a thousand years, and together we sleep in peace, for we are not alone.